SHARE

ROMANCE IN NYC: DOUBLE DELIGHT BOOK THREE

ANGEL DEVLIN

CHAPTER ONE

Haley

It was official. I sucked. I sucked at sucking. And no doubt at sex itself. But definitely at sucking if my friend's faces were to be believed as I attempted to give a wine bottle a blow job.

"Oh, hell, Hayley. It's a blow job, not a bunch of fresh flesh at a zombie party," noted my roommate Kayla.

My face fell. "See. I told you." Being crap at coitus was no joke.

"Let me get my own situation sorted, and then,

Haley, I will teach you. We can use a dildo or a banana. Whichever. I will show you how to do a BJ right."

"Thank you."

"And I will tell you all about the birds and the bees. See if you are doing that right," Tiff, my ex-roommate and now next-door-neighbor added.

At that point, a knock came at the door. Kayla's mom had come to see her about a tense situation she had just left. Kayla had come over tonight from Daniel, her ex-stepfather's house because she had started a relationship with him and a guy called Parker, her mom's new stepson. Here I was with no man in my life and Kayla had two!

Tiffany returned to the living room. Monday night was girls' night. Even though she now lived next door with her husband, Brandon, Monday's remained a man-free zone, rather like my pussy. "I hope they are going to be all right," Tiff stated, nodding toward the hallway. Kayla and her mom didn't have a great history.

I shrugged my shoulders. Kayla's mom had just walked into Daniel's home to find her, Daniel, and Parker in the throes of passion. "Well, we are here if not."

. . .

Kayla worked things out with her mom, and then also with Daniel and Parker, and the three of them were cohabiting in Port Jeff. Kayla had given notice on her share of the apartment and so this evening, her and Tiff were coming over to help me interview potential new roommates. I had jokingly said I wanted two hot males, but to be honest, as long as the newbies didn't look like serial killers or other such weirdos, I would be happy. Good references were key to getting a key. My apartment had three bedrooms. Mine, at the front, had an en-suite. It over-looked the parking lot for the apartments, but beyond that and the street, there were nice views. We had all worked for Green's, a Realtors based in Brooklyn. Kayla had now left to join Daniel's art business. He was an artist, owned a gallery and was looking to expand. Tiff still worked at Green's but was plan-ning on trying for a baby with her husband, so I didn't know what her long-term plans were. I felt like the only one of us with no life. Maybe I should ask all the apartment applicants if they were boyfriend-less and downbeat? Make sure we had common ground. I tried to shake the melancholy hanging over me. I was pleased my friends were both in love, and as they kept on telling me, it would happen for me too, one day. In the meantime, I needed to get better at sex. I figured if I watched some porn that could help. Though Kayla and Tiff had promised to help, they were just too busy getting on with their own lives. Anyhow, they didn't have dicks. I kinda needed the real thing to practice on. I wondered about paying for a male escort, that was how bad things were getting.

Out of the three of us girls, I was by far the most innocent. Through college, I had dated Liam and he had been the guy to take my cherry. I had thought we were good together, but once we graduated, he graduated onto another girl. We had hardly ever had oral. He said he didn't like it, either the giving or receiving, so it wasn't until I started dating other guys that it all went wrong. I had not got past first base with many dates. I always got shy and clammed up. Having no idea what to converse about other than my friends and work, most dates didn't progress to a second. A couple times things had gone to the bedroom, it had been a disaster. My pussy was so dry men couldn't get near it. My latest date, another realtor from Green's, Malcolm, blamed me for the fact he had not been able to get it up. Truth was, my only real joy came from my other best friend, B.O.B., that's right, my battery operated boyfriend who never let me down. He was a bendable rabbit vibrator who I could position to hit my clit and my pussy at the same time.

I noticed the time and realized I needed a final flurry of domestic activity. The two bedrooms down the hall were where the two new roommates would be and there was a shared bathroom for them to use. Both rooms had been given a fresh lick of paint last week and thoroughly cleaned and aired. Each had a queen bed, fitted closet space, and a dresser. A TV was fixed to a wall in each, so they'd be able to escape to their rooms if they wanted each night. Butterflies hit my gut followed by a feeling of dread. What if they seemed nice, so I gave them a key and then we didn't get on at all? I shook my head and went through to my en-suite to shower before the girls arrived. We were having pizza after the interviews, so I grabbed a bag of potato chips to eat before I hit the shower. It was a shame I couldn't afford the apartment on my own. Peace and quiet could be nice at times and at least there would be no more witnesses to my dating disasters. By tonight I might have one or two new roommates. I crossed my fingers, closed my eyes and said pretty please.

.   .   .

"I am so freaking hungry. How long is this gonna take?" Kayla moaned. The redhead patted her svelte stomach and it emitted a gurgle.

"Yeah? Well, I might have had more sympathy if your hair didn't look all fucked up. You had sex before you came here, didn't you?"

"Might have." Kayla winked.

There was a noise from the vicinity of the unlocked front door, followed by a flurry of footsteps. "I'm not late. There's one minute to 6pm," Tiff announced like I hadn't been checking my wristwatch every thirty seconds since 5pm.

"Oh my god, not you too!"

"Not me too, what?"

"You have sex hair. I need to get laid. I need to learn sex and get laid."

Just then the doorbell rang.

"Take a seat, you two, for Christ's sake and straighten each other's hair. There is serious decision making to be done," I chastised them.

The interviews were a complete waste of time with just two people to go. We had interviewed a pregnant woman, who didn't announce she was pregnant even though her stomach kept moving. She kept repositioning her wrap. If she wasn't pregnant, she had weird medical problems, so she was out. The second woman we interviewed was clearly a call girl, asking if men were allowed back before I'd had a chance to ask her to confirm her name. The others seemed fine but had not shown that we had any common ground and after the fantastic apartment share I'd had with Tiff and Kayla, I was reluctant to settle for business people.

"Well, this looks like a complete bust," I said to Tiff and Kayla.

"Don't give up yet. There are two men to come. They might be the sex on legs you've been looking for," Tiff said.

"Of course they will, Tiff. Dreams like that come true all the time, especially with me. They will be two sex gods who want me as a filling in their sandwich. Now if we could all wake up, I am going to open a bottle of wine. Screw this."

Tiff went to answer the door to the next-to-last applicant while I stood in the kitchen in the corner of our apartment pouring a very large glass of red wine. I couldn't afford to keep the apartment going on my own, so if these next two weren't of any use, then it looked like business bores were moving in with me. I took a secret large swig of wine with my back to the room and then turned around where I choked and spat red wine straight down my white blouse. For fuck's sake!

In front of me and stood at the side of Tiff, were two of the most gorgeous men I had ever laid eyes on. Seriously, if Victoria's Secret ever had a brother business called Victor's Secret with men modeling boxer shorts, these two needed to be included. In fact, in my head, that was all I could see.

"Erm, Haley. You have an, erm, strawberry cordial situation going on," Kayla said. "Take a seat, you guys, while we get sorted. Haley had the hiccoughs." She gave me a steely gaze, and I knew better than to say anything. I jolted out of my daydreams, back to the reality of my surroundings and blushed to the roots of my hair. I had red wine dripping down my chin and it was all down my blouse.

"Hi." I decided to add to the charade by doing a hiccough, then I headed for the sink.

"What on earth are you doing? Best behavior. You need these two in your life," hissed Kayla.

I sponged my blouse down, dried it the best I could and sat back down.

"Sorry about that, erm—"

"Chase. Chase Collins."

I stood and held out a hand for him to shake. "Pleased to meet you." I took in Chase's vivid blue eyes and his smile. He had short, blond hair. I'd put him at about six feet tall. At the side of my small frame, he was a giant.

Tiffany turned to me. "And this is your last applicant too, Todd Ross. They are friends and so thought they would attend together."

My mouth dropped open. "Oh, friends, that is so cool. How long y'all been friends for?"

"A couple of years now," Todd said. "We met at work." Again, I spent a moment taking in the appearance of my potential new roommate. Todd was dark haired; olive-skinned; and had deep, dark-brown eyes. He looked like that actor from Lucifer.

Realizing I had been staring, I looked at my list of questions. "And what do you do for an occupation?"

Chase looked across at Todd, who nodded. "We run an adult entertainment company."

"Like paintball?" I asked.

Kayla snorted which I didn't think was amusing or professional.

"No, we film adult movies."

"Porn?" My mouth dropped open again.

"Yes. If you want to call it that," Chase said. "We run a small, reputable company which is like a little family."

"Wow, I bet that is so interesting," Tiff said. "I bet you have a few stories to share."

"We certainly do," Todd replied. His eyes twinkled as he smiled. I couldn't let these two move in. I would be hopeless. I would probably keep forgetting to move. In fact, I would win the record for the longest mannequin challenge while I ogled these two all day.

I managed to conduct myself for the rest of the interview in what I hoped was a professional manner. Then I showed them around and thanked them for coming.

"I have a few applicants to consider, but I will let you know later this evening," I told them. It was very hard to not jump up and down and ask them when they could both move in.

"Not a problem," Chase said. "We will leave you to the rest of your... strawberry cordial..."

I followed his gaze to the kitchen countertop where the opened bottle of wine was on clear display.

I looked back at Chase, and he smirked. He was a cheeky one, this guy. I liked him already.

"Strawberry cordial is the best," I replied. Then I showed them out of the door.

"Oh my fucking god, they were scrumilicious," I shrieked. "I can't live with them."

"Why not?" Tiff's face had hardened into a frown.

"I mean how am I going to live with them? I'll be permanently in my room with my vibe!"

"They met at work. I wonder if they met behind the camera or in front of it?" Kayla asked.

"You mean they might do the porn?" For the bazillionth time that day my jaw hung open. I was going to need a physician for lockjaw if I carried on.

"Could have started that way. You will have to ask them once they live here," she added. "You need to phone them, like now, before they look anywhere else. They are sexy as fuck and they can help teach you sex by showing you their movies. They might even let you visit the set and get some hands-on experience." Kayla chuckled wickedly.

Taking my cell from my purse, I called the

number Chase had given me and asked if he and Todd fancied being my roommates.

Walking back into the kitchen, I drank some more red wine. "I did it. Jeez, I fucking did it," I told the girls. "I got two hot as fuck male roommates. Now get the pizza ordered. We need to celebrate."

CHAPTER TWO

Haley

I was amazed at how fast we all settled into the new arrangement. The guys worked long hours and often called to see if I wanted takeout. They were going to make me fat. I already had an ass larger than Kim Kardashian's. If they didn't stop feeding me, I was gonna be as wide as I was tall, being as I was only a little over five feet. Chase was a talker. I reckoned I knew his whole life story by now and that of Todd too, as Chase had no filter and just said everything he thought. He was so cheeky with it though. His blue eyes sparkled when he said something risqué. Todd wasn't quiet either, though he struggled to get a word in edge-ways with Chase. Often, he rolled his eyes at me and shook his head. It was nice then on times like tonight when Todd was home and Chase still working and I got to talk with him a little more.

"So, tell me more about how you started GoDown Movies," I asked him while trying to capture noodles with chopsticks. Chase had given a very speedy version of events, seeing as he ran at the mouth, but I wanted to know the full version.

"Simple really. I was working as an attorney and had to assist a company with the legal side of getting their business started. I saw how the big players in the porn world didn't take kindly to anyone muscling in on that territory. Came across a few guys I would rather keep on my good side. I learned it could be pretty lucrative as long as you didn't overstep. So, I set my own small business up, that didn't threaten any of the big players. Soon I didn't need to be an attorney anymore, which was twisting my balls. I had met Chase via the other company; he was a camera-man. We had had drinks a few times and hit it off, both of us wanting to make money, and he left the other fledgling business and joined in my enterprise. We never looked back. By keeping it small, we are left to get on with it."

"God, it sounds dangerous, like the mob or something."

"It's like any business, you have competition. With the adult entertainment industry, some of the bigger players send in the heavies if you are taking money or models away from them. We've learned how to work alongside them; we're no threat and they leave us alone. We reckon we will only need to work for about another five years and we should be financially set. Then we are done. It will be time to look around for the perfect woman and do the whole having kids bit."

"Wow, sounds like you have it all worked out," I said, wishing my own life had any hint of a happy future in it.

"It's all still dreams at the moment, Haley. Gotta have dreams."

"I have nightmares instead," I told him.

"How so? You're a beautiful woman. How come there is no Mr. Haley?" Todd's eyes fixed on me with that dark, brooding stare and I kinda lost my train of thought for a second.

"I don't have any luck with men. Tiff and Kayla are trying to help me. I can't really say why, because it's embarrassing."

"I wouldn't say anything, Haley. I know we have

only been roomies for a couple of months, but you can talk to me."

I sighed. "I suck at sex."

Todd almost choked on a noodle.

"Why on earth would you think that?"

"I've been told several times. Even Kayla and Tiffany seem to have given up on me as I can't get the hang of practicing blow jobs on bananas. I hate bananas."

I realized Todd was almost puce in the face and I couldn't work out if that was because of my declaration or because of his almost choking. I got up and got him a glass of water which was gratefully received.

"Sorry," I told him. "I tend to overshare."

"No, I asked. I just wasn't expecting you to say that."

"Well, Tiff wondered whether you might let me watch filming some time, so I can get an idea; but I'll be honest, I've watched pornos and I don't know how the women bob up and down like that."

"You can't learn from porn, it's unrealistic. We have all sorts of tricks of the trade and most people don't conduct their sex lives like that."

"You say that, but Kayla lives in a polyamorous

relationship, and Tiffany had threesomes with her husband and a man who owns a sex club."

"Did someone say sex club?" Chase walked through the door. "Where, and when are we going?"

"You need a beer, buddy?" Todd asked. "Even you are going to be rendered speechless by what Haley has to tell you."

Chase threw his jacket on the floor in the center of the room, walked over to the fridge where he grabbed a beer, and with the bottle opened, he sprawled across the couch with his feet up.

"Tell me everything." he said. I swear the guy should work for the National Enquirer.

"I have only heard a shortened version of the 'my roommates like threesomes'," Todd added. "Seriously, I figure we could make a movie about Haley, the innocent roommate."

"Screw you," I said and flounced into the kitchen area where I grabbed a bottle of wine.

"You drove her to strawberry cordial, dude," Chase yelled.

I gave him the finger.

"Come on, tell Chase everything." He patted the couch in front of him, indicating a space near his chest. I walked over and thought 'what the hell' and sat down, resting my back against his midriff. His body heat soaked into my skin. I had an urge to snuggle.

"Which bit do you want to know? The I'm hopeless at sex bit, or the gossip about my ex-roommates' romantic lives?"

"Both but start with the roommates. So, they didn't just leave because they fell in love?"

"Well, they did, but they both had awesome, amazing sexcapades."

"Aww, honey. You sound jealous." Chase sat up and pulled me under his arm. I thought I would die of lust as his toned arm wrapped around me and he pulled my head under his chin, stroking my hair. "You will get laid, sweetheart. It will happen. No need to be embarrassed about still being a virgin."

I knocked his arm off me. "I am not a virgin. I am just awful at sex."

Chase looked at me and smirked.

"Stop tormenting her, Chase, or she will withhold the gossip," Todd threatened.

"Sorry, Haley." Chase tried his hardest to make a contrite face but the smirk at the corner of his mouth remained.

"Do you want to know about Kayla and Tiffany?" I asked.

"Totally, yes," Chase answered.

"Then give your mouth a break and your ears a turn."

Todd laughed, a great hearty rumble erupting from his throat. "You've been told." He went to get himself a beer and made himself comfortable in the chair near the couch.

"Okay, so Tiff first. None of the girls hide anything, so I'm not telling you anything I shouldn't. She works for Green's like me and one day she got an email from a mystery guy called H. It said all this stuff he wanted to do to her, you know, dirty stuff. She thought it was from a creep and then she went to show a condo and the businessman was H. His name's Henry Carter and he owns a sex club called Club S.

"Club S? Yeah, we've been there. I might open a Club O, that's the one everyone would wanna visit."

Todd rolled his eyes.

"Anyhow, Brandon moved in next door and he and Tiffany fell in love, but they ended up having threesomes for a while with H. Meanwhile, I couldn't land one guy."

Chase and Todd exchanged glances.

"I know. You want me to carry on. Okay, so then there is Kayla who'd had a crush on her stepfather for-ev-er, except he wasn't really sorta her stepfather because it turned out he and her mother were never together, if you get me, and then she goes to visit him, and Parker is there, her mom's new stepson and she starts a relationship with both of them. Here I am again with no one, I repeat no one, and they have both had two guys."

I then realized I was shouting this fact out to two hot guys and clamped my mouth shut, because what if they thought I was hinting. I kinda hoped they thought I was hinting.

"Anyhow, Tiffany moved in with Brandon and they got married; Kayla moved in with Daniel and Parker a few months back; and now I have you guys to be my new roommates who have to listen to my tales of woe in the dating department."

"I don't remember that being on the lease," Todd added, with a wink.

"Small print. So tiny ya can't see it," I replied.

"So, onto you and your 'tales of woe'," Chase said.

"Okay." I shuffled myself closer to Chase. "I have only had one full on lover and he said I was a pretty bad lover. I thought he was just being bitter when we broke up, but since then when I have gone past first base with other guys, I have either had radio silence afterward, or they tell me I can't perform blow jobs properly. The guy I dated last, another realtor from Greens said I was the reason he couldn't get it up."

"That's bullshit. My dick often goes stiff in your presence, Haley," Chase added.

"Chase. For God's sake," Todd said.

He shrugged. "It's true. Yours does too; tell her."

I held my hand up. "That's okay, Todd." I leaned over and hugged Chase. "But thank you, Chase, for trying to help."

"See, now you made it happen again."

I looked at him horrified and moved a little further away.

"Joking! Oh, girl, you are so cute. Seriously, these guys who you've been dating. They are losers. They are making shit up to cover their own failings."

I shook my head. "Maybe, but there is truth in it. Kayla had me demonstrate a blow job on a bottle. I was hopeless. You should have seen their faces. Complete disbelief. She told Tiffany that she had to teach me with either bananas or dildos. I chose bananas and I bought my own because you never know what is happening around their apartment." I pulled a face.

"So, what happened?" Chase asked.

"I still suck at blow jobs, and I now hate bananas."

"Oh, girl, you need to get some proper practice. You can't learn how to suck a guy on a banana. Our man parts aren't fruit, although my ass is kinda peachy," Chase added.

"She wanted to come watch a movie being made," Todd said. "To learn."

"We will take you to watch one sometime, but that is not how you learn. Now, here, take my beer bottle. Show me. It can't have been that bad."

I took the bottle from him and wrapped my mouth around it like Tiff had said to do, then tried to hollow out my cheeks and suck.

"Oh my god, it's like a puffer fish," Chase exclaimed.

"I told you. I suck at sucking," I yelled. Then I stormed out of the room, slamming the door behind me.

I sat back on my own bed, tears welling in the corner of my eyes. I had done my damnedest to be a good girl my whole life. Never did drugs, passed my exams by studying hard. I deserved to be able to have a damn good fucking. It wasn't fair. My rabbit made me feel things my first boyfriend, Liam, never had, so I knew there was more out there to experience. I just needed to do it. Maybe I would have to ask Henry for a membership to Club S. I could wear a mask and ask men if I could suck their cocks. At least if I was useless at it, they wouldn't see my face, and hey, practice made perfect, right? I decided that after work that next day I would ask Tiffany if she was still in touch with Henry and to get me a membership card.

The next morning, I apologized to the guys. I hoped I hadn't put them off as tenants by being such a girl. I grabbed a coffee in my takeout cup, stuck a slice of toast in between my teeth, and headed out for Green's. I was hoping to get a good bonus this month as there was a pair of five-inch Ferragamo's with my name on them. When you're short like me, heels are everything, and these were everything and more. They were a high heel pump with a black ankle strap and a see-through mesh body with a matching trim.

I headed through the door of the office. Green's was a glass-fronted building located on 7th Avenue. I said good morning to the reception staff and strolled through to my part of the large open-plan office. Deciding I needed more stimulation before I attacked the day, I went into the staff room and pressed the necessary buttons to ensure a perfect latte emerged from the expensive coffee machine in situ.

"Morning, Haley." I turned around to see Malcolm had just come in. Malcolm of the disastrous 'I can't get it up and it's all your fault', date.

"Malcolm," I said tersely. I really didn't want to speak to him.

"Haley." He walked in front of me, so I had no choice but to look at him. He was around five feet ten, slim built, with ash-blond hair and green eyes. His eyes were nice, they looked kindly, which kinda sucked. That's why I had said yes to a date. Shame he was an asshole.

"Sorry, do you want to get to the coffee machine?" I grabbed my drink and backed away.

"No." He placed a hand on my arm. "I wanted to apologize. For when we went out. I was an idiot and not a gentleman. I was embarrassed, you know. I- I've never had that happen to me before. So I blamed you. It was bad form and I'm sorry. I'm also sorry it has taken me so long to come and apologize to you."

"It hurt me, Malcolm. I felt embarrassed too. Like I was less of a woman, you know."

"That's how I felt, Haley, less of a man. I really am so, so sorry. Please, could I take you out again?"

I opened my mouth to protest, but he interrupted.

"Just dinner. To a really nice restaurant. We can talk, get to know each other. Please. Let me take you out and spoil you. You deserve it. I want you to see that is not who I really am."

I sighed and closed my eyes for a moment. I did enjoy eating and here was a free dinner. I opened my eyes. "Okay. Dinner only. I will not be coming back to yours."

"Well, maybe another time we might try again, but for now, dinner. Fantastic. I will pick you up at eight?"

I nodded and then took my coffee back out to the office. We had a large apartment development coming up to sell soon and I needed to spend some time working on my sales pitch if I was to land it for my portfolio. I looked down at my feet and admired my Jimmy Choos. *I won't abandon you*, I promised them. You just have to learn to share.

"You're doing what? Going out with that asshole again? Over my dead body, Haley Martin."

I had never seen Chase angry before, but he

looked like he was going to punch a wall. "Todd," he shouted down the hall. "Get out here now."

Todd emerged from his room out into the hallway, rubbing his eyes. "I was having a nap. What's going on?"

"Haley here, has decided to go on another date with floppy dick."

"His name is Malcolm."

"I can't think of anything that goes with an M, all right? So I have named his penis instead."

"You named another man's penis?"

"Yes, and it is not the first time. Is it Todd?"

Todd shook his head, "It really isn't."

"Cancel, and we will take you out instead," Todd said, looking at Chase for his approval.

"Yes, let us take you out. We're much more fun," Chase agreed.

"Thanks, guys, but it is just dinner. He is taking me out because he wants to say sorry for what happened, that's all. It's just to clear the air. I'm going because it has made work awkward, so I need to do this, okay?"

"I am not happy," Chase replied. "Do not give him anything. Not any tongue, or a hand job. Nothing."

"Yes, all right. I won't anyway in case I give him another reason to tell me I'm hopeless in bed."

"Go on your date, lady. Sorry, on your dinner. We are not even calling this a date, and then straight home. We'll be having a chat tomorrow about this whole," he flamboyantly wafted his hand all the way down the front of me but did an extra couple of circles near my pussy, "situation."

I sighed. "Fine, but right now I am going to get ready for my dinner." I left them in the hall and returned to my room. They were more trouble and more dramatic than the girls.

CHAPTER THREE

Haley

Malcolm had chosen a steakhouse on 84th Street. When he was due to come pick me up, I had waited outside, rather than let Chase be in shouting distance of him. Malcolm's eyes had trailed down my body and I was about to call him on it, when he informed me I was probably overdressed for where we were going.

When he had said he was taking me for an apology dinner to a nice restaurant, I had wrongly anticipated a nice little Italian like we had gone to on our first date, so the steakhouse had taken me by surprise. Don't get me wrong, I loved eating in any place, but I wished he would have given me a heads up on the location of dinner. I had on a little black dress and heels and wished I could tap my shoes Dorothy style and be in a pair of jeans and a checked button down, with sneakers on my feet.

We ordered two porterhouses on the green, and Malcolm ordered a beer while I asked for water. I wanted to keep a clear head and make sure I didn't fall for any of his sales bullshit. He was a good realtor and that sales charm extended outside of work.

Within five minutes of being there, I once again wished for sneakers, so I could run the hell home. We had shared about three sentences of conversation and the subject of the weather was completely exhausted.

I took a sip of my water and looked around the restaurant. There were couples and families, all engaged in conversation. They wore happy smiles on their faces while they tucked into their food. I wanted that. I wanted to be in a restaurant with my significant others, having a great time. Not stuck here with Malcolm. God, please let my steak get here soon, so I could make my excuses and leave.

"So, about the last time we got together—"

"It's okay, really."

"No, look. I wanted to say. It had been a while for me."

"Oh, okay."

"So, that is probably part of why we had trouble that night, as well as, you know."

I felt my neck tense up. "As well as what?"

"Never mind."

At that point, the waitress delivered our steaks and mine looked so mouth-wateringly delicious that I didn't question Malcolm any further because I didn't want to stab him to death with my steak knife and be prevented from eating my food.

"What do you think about the development of King Park on the Upper East Side?" Malcolm asked. That was the new development I had been trying to get for my portfolio and no doubt a hungry salesman like Malcolm wanted it too.

"It looks great. I'm sure we'll sell most of the apartments off plan, given the location."

Malcolm rambled on about how amazing for families it would be. Personally, I didn't agree. I thought it would make a great place for wealthy busi-nessmen to install their mistresses in a home from home when they were in New York on business, but I wasn't going to share my views. I finished my steak, wiped my mouth with a napkin and sat back.

"Would you like a dessert?" he asked.

"No, thank you, Malcolm. I'm feeling beat. If it's okay with you, I'd like to go home now."

"Before you go…"

"Yeah?" I sighed.

"I have a proposition for you."

I started to get up from the table before he tried to get in my pants again.

"It's about Green's."

When I realized it was about business, I relaxed and turned to him.

"What's that?"

"I thought we could partner up on King Park. We could be a killer team, Haley. We're both great at sales and we're both hot. You can flirt with the husbands, and me the wives, right?"

I was simply speechless. Was this man for real?

"Then I thought we could extend our partnership back home." He winked. He actually fucking winked at me. "I figure I'll have no problems from here on out, and I don't mind giving you a few pointers on technique."

Thank goodness I had not finished my carafe of water because it was in easy reach and gave me much more satisfaction dripping down Malcolm's face than it would have my throat. I most definitely preferred red wine.

"You arrogant ass," I screamed.

Malcolm's eyes swept around the restaurant, noting the faces of the people who had stopped eating and were now our captive audience.

"I will land King Park by myself and as for your limp hot-dog, (I was mindful there were children listening), find another roll for it because it is certainly not getting eaten by me." I threw money on the table to cover my portion of the bill because there was no way I was owing the guy anything, then I turned on my heel and stomped out, waving down a cab and heading back to my own apartment far earlier than I had envisioned. I had really wanted a sundae too.

It wasn't even 10pm and yet the lights were out at the front of the apartment. Looked like Chase and Todd might have gone out too. I was glad. It meant I could sulk on the couch for a couple hours and watch a movie, preferably something where a godawful guy got beaten to death. I opened the door of the apartment and saw a light was on in Chase's room. Did he ever turn them off and think about the environment? I hung my jacket, dropped my purse in the hallway and walked down to his room to turn it off. Then I heard moaning. I stopped in my tracks. Shit. Did Chase have a woman in his room?

Then I heard Chase's voice, as clear as day, yell out, "Fuck, Todd, I'm coming."

What the hell?

I tiptoed down the hall. My mind yelled at me to go back to my room, but my body propelled me forward. I stared through the crack between the door and the door jamb and my heart thudded at the scene in front of me. Todd was laid across Chase's chest, his cock in his hand. His dick was huge, with thick veins, and was an angry purple as if it was desperate to explode. Chase's dick laid at the side of his leg, cum smeared on it after he had clearly just shot his load. I knew I should back away, this was private, but I was in shock. How had I not realized they were a couple? Had they deliberately tried to conceal it from me, or was I just that goddamn naive and stupid I hadn't noticed what was in front of my face? I was certainly noticing what was in front of my face now. Two cocks. I examined Chase's. Though it was currently not erect, it appeared a decent size and was quite wide. Two huge dicks. They were lucky guys. I stayed by the doorway as Todd reached over to grab a bottle of lube. He tipped some out into his hand and then coated his dick. Then he lowered himself further down and lining his cock with Chase's ass, he thrust forward into Chase's puckered hole. Chase gasped, his face contorting in ecstasy as he placed his hand back on his own cock, which stirred into life. I watched the men in front of me fuck: Todd thrusting away until sweat beaded his forehead, Chase's head hitting the headboard with each thrust. They were caught in a frenzied fuck until with a shout Todd reached his release, filling Chase's ass with his cum. Then he shuffled right off the end of the bed and took Chase's cock in his mouth where he sucked it until Chase came again, swallowing his load and licking his lips. I quietly backed away, not wanting to intrude on any intimacy. What I had done, spying on them like that was bad enough. I tiptoed back to my own room, where I stripped off my clothes, wiped the makeup from my face and hit the shower. In the privacy of my own bathroom, away from the other bedrooms, and with the shower masking any sounds, I let the tears fall, while I reached some kind of high level of hysteria. Not only was I so bad in bed people felt they had to offer me lessons, but I was the only woman in the world who could get herself two hot roommates and discover they were gay. I sat on the floor of the shower while water cascaded down me and sobbed until I had nothing left to give.

When I eventually left the shower and toweled myself off, I put on my sleep shorts and cami, climbed under my comforter, and came to an agreement with myself. I would definitely see Tiffany tomorrow and contact Henry Carter. I was going to become the best fucking fuck there was. A blow job queen, and nothing was going to stop me. Haley Martin was not going to take this lying down I thought, then I realized that yes, I probably was. That thought made me smile and with that, I fell asleep.

Usually, on a Saturday I still got up early so I could make the most of the day, but this morning I stayed in bed and waited until I heard Chase and Todd leave. They had started going to Brandon's gym as he had promised to help them develop a fitness regime, and Saturday mornings were a day they could stick to. It also meant I knew that Tiffany was probably at home. She may have become a gym bunny with a fitness instructor husband, but I knew she was a lazybones and was no doubt currently making the most of being able to starfish in bed.

I got out of bed, wrapped myself in my robe, added bed socks to my ensemble because my feet were like ice, and then I padded down the hall and into our living space where I headed for the kitchen and set up the coffee machine for some fresh heaven in a mug. I grabbed my phone from the side and saw I had a message.

Malcolm: You embarrassed yourself last night. You owe me an apology.

Was he serious? I felt my temper build again. I hit Tiff's number and listened to it ring.

"Mmmmph."

"Tiff. Code red."

There was a muffled response which sounded akin to 'hold on' and then I heard bedlinen rustle.

"What is it, girl. Who do I need to kill?"

"Can I come round? I'm still in my sleep shorts. I'll bring coffee."

"I'll leave the door unlocked. Lock it behind you. You will find me under the comforter."

I made two coffees and put them in reusable

cups from a local coffee shop chain and went around next door. Pushing open the door, I was always surprised at how similar their apartment was to ours. The only difference being theirs was a two bed apartment.

I pushed open Tiff's bedroom door. I could just see a bird's nest of blonde hair poking out of the top of the comforter.

I put her coffee on her nightstand and got on the top of the covers and huddled next to her.

Tiff emerged slowly, an inch at a time until her head was visible. Then she sat up and grabbed her coffee from the nightstand.

"So, code red, huh?"

"Yes. Like the quote I saw on Pinterest last week, it would appear rock bottom has a basement."

She placed an arm around me. "What's happened, honey?"

"I went on another date with Malcolm."

"You did what?" she screeched.

"I know, I know. He said he wanted to take me to dinner to apologize for his behavior last time. Really, he just wanted to feel me out for my secrets on King Park. He wants to muscle in on the development he knows I will get. I have worked my ass off, there's no way he is getting his hands on it. Especially not now, the limp-dick."

"Oh dear. So another unsuccessful date?"

"Well, one of us ended up wet, but it wasn't me, and it was courtesy of a carafe of water."

Tiff burst out laughing.

"Good for you. I'm not seeing why this is a code red though. You already knew the guy was a dick."

"I came home and discovered Chase and Todd fucking."

"Oh."

"Yes, indeed, oh."

"So, that must have been embarrassing for you all?"

"They don't know I saw. I spied on them through the crack in the door, like a voyeur. Seriously, I couldn't avert my gaze."

"So is it hot seeing two guys together?"

"Tiff! Are you not listening to me? My roomies are gay. Gay! The roommates I chose with a potential apartment orgy in mind are gay. Not only do I get no sexy times, but I have to hear them at it!"

"It's not that bad."

"Not that bad? Sure, perhaps they could move Malcolm in and then all three could go at it while he tells me their cocks get him hard."

Another round of laughter burst from Tiff.

"God, you are not taking this seriously. I'm hurting Tiff. I came by for sympathy. You don't even sound surprised. Was it obvious to you they were together? Is it just me with no gaydar? Anyway, I need you to get in touch with H for me."

Tiff sat up straight in bed. Holding a hand up at me to get me to be quiet, she took a large gulp of her coffee before placing it back on the bedside table. "H? Henry? Why do you want me to contact him?"

"I want a membership to Club S. Do they have nights where they wear masks? I need to go in without anyone knowing who I am, so I can practice sex and sucking cock."

"Seriously, there is no need, Hales."

"No need! You are hearing about my sad, desperate love life, aren't you?"

"Yes, and that's why I gave your apartment details to Chase and Todd."

My hand flew to my chest and I gasped.

"What? You gave them my details? You knew I wanted hot guys and stuck me with two gay men?"

"They are not gay, they are bisexual. They like pussy too."

"Fuck this coffee's strong. I swear you just said you set me up with bisexual roommates," I yelled.

"Calm down. Yes, I did. I knew you wanted some hot roommates and I'd seen your applicants. There weren't any. So I called Henry and asked him if he knew anyone who was looking for a place. He put out feelers and came back with Chase and Todd. They are looking for a permanent partner. A female. They are together, have been for a while, but as I said, they like pussy too and they are thinking of the future and potentially having a family.

My mouth did its usual jaw drop. Seriously, I was going to need plastic surgery for saggy skin around my jaw if this kept up.

"What the, erm..."

"I'm sorry, Hales. I know this must be a shock, but I was thinking of what you said. There is no pressure. Chase and Todd were looking for an apartment, but they didn't move in expecting you to be part of the arrangement. They planned on looking around and then moving when they found someone. I was just wanting for you to have the option. That is if maybe you liked them and they you... well, it could work out. Or at least give you some practice."

"I seriously, like don't know what to think. I forgot I'd been asking advice from Mrs. Tiff Three-way-I-went-out-on-stage-and-had-sex-with-an-audi-ence-watching Bailey. So, get a hot roomie Haley.

Why stop there? Get two roomies, hell, make them bisexual and wanting a female as a trio. Is there some three-way club you and Kayla joined and now you're co-opting me or something?"

Tiff smiled. The girl could have been offended but she was so happy she didn't give a crap about my outburst.

"Hey, I know how much fun it can be. I got it out of my system, but look at Kayla. She's in it for life. Normal dating isn't working out so well for you, so why not try this?"

"So, what do I do? Just go home and say, 'hey guys, I saw you fucking and well I would like to join in, can I have a sample. Is there an audition?'."

"Well, not quite like that, but I would tell them you saw them and just open a dialogue. Ask them about themselves. They are really open according to Henry. I figured they would have told you soon about themselves anyway once you were all settled."

I sat back and thought about what I had just learned. Tiff yawned so wide she nearly broke her jaw. I crawled under the comforter. "Okay, I'm staying for a nap. My mind has exploded. Put the alarm on for in a couple hours."

"Oh, thank Christ, I'm beat," Tiff said and with that, we both fell asleep.

. . .

"Oh, Tiffany, all my dreams have come true. Are we having a threesome with Haley?"

Tiff had failed to set an alarm and it was now early afternoon and Brandon had returned from his classes. He stood in the doorway and took his tee off revealing a muscled torso and corded arms. She was a lucky girl, but even if he had been serious, there was no way I was doing anything with a) my friend's husband, and b) girls. No thank you.

Tiffany leaped out of bed and threw her arms around her husband. "Missed you, baby."

"Missed you too. I'm just going to hit the shower."

I took one look at my friend's face and launched myself out of bed. "I am off back to mine. Thanks for the chat, Tiff. Good to see you, Brandon. Now it looks like your wife wants to join you in the shower, so I am leaving before you guys do something in front of me that makes me want to vomit."

"And there I was thinking you liked to watch after last night," Tiff quipped.

"What about last night?" Brandon asked.

"Shut it, Tiff, and Brandon, never you mind,

although Tiff's mouth is so big, no doubt you'll know before I've even left."

"Hey, I have no complaints about her big mouth. She needs it for my big—"

I placed my hands over my ears, "Lalalalala." I reversed out of the room and left. I'd get my coffee cups back later. For now, I made my escape.

CHAPTER FOUR

Haley

My mind was reeling.

Bisexual roommates.

Hot roommates.

Threesomes.

The fact Tiff had engineered this on purpose.

Would Chase and Todd see me as a potential lover? I would seriously doubt it given I had told them how hopeless in bed I was. It was like winning the booby prize on a chat show and even then, I only had a small handful—what should have gone to my breasts had wandered off and accidentally added to my ass.

I hated my inexperience. At twenty-four I should know what I was doing.

I crawled back into my own bed. There was no sign of the guys and stuck for anything else to do that wasn't a chore, I powered up my laptop, positioned it on its laptop cushion and went to a porn site that Kayla never stopped raving about. I typed in two men and one woman and a host of videos displayed. I kept seeing the words MMF and MFM so I went onto Google to find out what the definitions stood for. I quickly discovered that MFM was like what Kayla and Tiffany had experienced, a threesome where the guys didn't get involved with each other; but MMF was everyone involved with each other, so as well as fucking the female they'd have sex with each other too, do blow jobs, etc. The videos were rated and so I chose one with a high percentage which hopefully meant it was good and sat back and watched.

In this video, a couple: one man, and one woman had advertised for a male partner to join them. It wasn't long before everyone's clothes were off. In the beginning, the woman laid back on the bed while one man licked her pussy and another thrust his cock down her throat. I felt my legs pulse and my pussy instantly got wet. The man withdrew his cock and started sucking on her breasts. Hands, mouths, and cocks were everywhere. I started to see why Kayla and Tiff had been so into their threesomes. This was HOT. Then, as one man started to fuck the woman, he leaned over and took the other guy's cock in his mouth. My heart beat faster. It was so erotic! I was surprised at myself. Why was the thought of a man with another man turning me on? I couldn't explain it, but I wasn't about to stop watching! They switched around again and this time the woman was being fucked in the pussy by a guy who was himself getting fucked in the ass. I moved my hand down my pajama shorts and started flicking my nub as I watched. I wanted to watch another scene with a woman getting her pussy eaten so I clicked on another clip. Once it got to a scene where a man was between her legs while another man fucked him from behind, I frantically rubbed at my clit while two fingers from my other hand pistoned inside my pussy. I tried not to be distracted by the fact that the laptop was jiggling up and down on my lap while I did it. I was pleased there was no one home, so that when I came, I screamed out loud as the tension I'd been holding dissipated from my body and left me in some kind of come-coma.

"Sounds like someone is having a good time." Chase's voice came from the hallway.

"Yeah, she must have brought the guy home. He is obviously very good at apologizing," Todd added.

My face flamed red. Oh my fucking God, they'd heard me and there was no one else in here. I was going to have to lie and somehow fake I'd just snuck him out of the apartment.

I quickly showered and then I left my room walking over to the apartment door, opening it and yelling, "Yeah, see you again sometime." Then I closed the door with a slam, so my roommates could hear it. I walked through to the living area and stretched like I'd had a great evening. I hated lying but there was no way I wanted them to know I had been solo when I'd climaxed like a singer practicing scales.

"Some mighty skills your guy has there, Haley. The power to make you screech like a freight train and then invisibility. Is it a cloak like in Harry Potter?"

Chase was staring out of the front window.

I tilted my chin up at him. "He jogs. He got out of here in no time."

"That may have worked if Chase hadn't been looking out of the window for the last ten minutes as he thinks the mailwoman is fit," Todd added. "Don't be ashamed about enjoying your body, Haley. We all do it. Perhaps your confidence would grow if you owned your body a little more. We are all adults. Chase and I don't care."

"Yeah, about that," I answered, seeing an opportunity to divert attention away from myself, "Last night when I got back home, I heard you two."

"Ah," Todd said. "Looks like we could use a chat. Shall we order pizza? I'm ravenous."

"You don't have anything to explain. I just wanted to let you know that I knew and that I am totally cool with all that, anything at all, any scenario you have going down."

Chase looked bemused, a smirk quirked his lip. "Like what? We didn't have animals in there or torture equipment."

I blushed again. "I don't know. Anything men do together, or if they have a woman in there as well. I am cool with it all. Go for it."

Todd walked over and folded me in his arms. I only reached his chest and so my face was smushed into his rock-hard pecs. I didn't want to move. "Oh, Haley. I might not have known you very long, but, babe, I adore you. You are so entirely sweet and endearing and innocent."

"I find it a problem myself," I mumbled into his chest.

"I'm going to order pizza and then we'll crack open some beer. For fuck's sake don't tell Brandon, after we just worked out with him. He was advising us to eat poached salmon and a side salad for lunch."

I giggled. "Your secret is safe with me as long as we get pepperoni."

"Blackmail, hey?" Chase added. "Well, this time I'll allow it seeing as you now know Todd and myself both like to eat meat."

"Oh my god, you didn't just say that." Todd covered my ears. "Don't listen to him, he's disgusting."

"Yeah, that's not what you were saying last night," Chase quipped. "Now while I order the pizza, Todd you get the beers, and Haley, please set the table."

I was pleased to note that rather than my operatic orgasm making me uncomfortable around the two men, now that they knew I knew they were a couple, everything was actually more relaxed. It was like a barrier had been broken through and we could talk about anything. I loved it because it was similar to the relationship I had with the girls, but now I was getting a male perspective on things, something I sorely needed.

When I told them about Malcolm they went insane.

"I am coming to your work. I am going to kick him in the balls," Chase said.

"If you need me to have a word, Haley, just say it and I'll be there. Only I'll use words rather than physical violence." Todd rolled his eyes in Chase's direction.

"No. I will get my revenge. I am going to get that development and rub his face in it when I make a huge commission."

"You need a goal, other than to beat Malcolm," Todd said. "Something to aim for. What do you want to get with the money?"

I explained about the shoes.

"Fuck the fuck-me heels. You can have those, but you're going to earn megabucks. What's something huge you want to aim for?" Chase asked.

I sat back for a moment resting against the back of the couch. "I would really love to go on a vacation where you are at the edge of the ocean and you eat on the beach. What people have for honeymoons, except I'm not married. But I have no one to go with and I'm not doing that on my own. I just don't see why honeymooners should own that kind of vacay. I want to be spoiled and massaged."

"We will come with you, babe. We need a break," Chase declared, looking at Todd.

"Yeah, well, great that we have these full and frank discussions where everyone gets their say." Todd raised an eyebrow.

"So, I'll go with you on my own, honey." Chase mock-whispered.

"Now, I didn't say I wouldn't go. Did I?" Todd retorted. "I'd just like it if for once you discussed things with me before you went jumping in with both feet."

Chase waved a hand in front of his own face. "Do I ever do that?"

"No." Todd sighed. "You don't. I am wasting my breath." Then he smiled at me. "You get that bonus, darlin', and we will go on that vacation with you."

I leaped up and hugged each of them in turn. "You guys are amazing, thank you."

The pizza arrived and we sat stuffing our faces. Thankfully, Brandon was obviously too busy in bed with Tiff to notice the arrival of the high calorie delivery.

"So how long have you two been together?" I asked when we were all laid back in various places around the living room rubbing our stomachs. I was on the couch, Todd was laid across the chair, and Chase was lying across the floor.

"Two years," Todd said. "We met at work. Both had girlfriends at the time. We hit it off as buddies and went on a double-date. Not long afterwards we realized we preferred each other to our girlfriends."

"I'd had both male and female partners before," Chase added. "But Todd was straight until then."

"I'd been curious, but not done anything," Todd said. "I was confused because I really liked pussy and found women attractive. I knew you could be bisexual, but kind of didn't believe it. I thought you would be more one thing than another. That it was a confused mind rather than a perfectly normal thing."

"So, we have had a committed relationship with each other, as in no more male partners in the last eighteen months, but we have had an open relationship where pussy is concerned," Chase added.

"But that is something else we are looking to change," Todd said. "We are going to look for a woman who can complete our relationship. Become part of a committed threesome. We know it could take time and it runs a risk of things not working out, but we would like a family someday—a stable family life—and that's where we see our future. We don't want to be out seeking pussy and the other one not involved. It doesn't seem right anymore." Todd looked at me intently. "I guess this is a lot to take in, right?"

"No, it's really not. I totally get it. It's a progression of your relationship to the next level that works for you. I applaud you for making such a great choice between you. You seem to have your shit together which is a lot more than other couples I know. Can I be honest about something?" The conversation and the beer in the afternoon had loosened my tongue.

"Sure," Todd said.

"I am really surprised but I find the thought of you two together, in general, a turn on. When I was in my room before, I was curious. I looked up some MMF. Tiff had told me a little already this morning about what you were looking for, so I kinda wanted to check out what it was about."

"Your 'little death' scream was at an MMF movie?" Chase's eyes widened.

"Yeah," I said, wondering why I'd confessed that and hoping I hadn't made things awkward.

Chase leaped up. "So, we think you're hot. Do you think you might try with us? Date us, with a view to it maybe leading to something else? I am more than willing to teach you about sex."

My mouth fell open and I bet my eyes bulged with shock. I was completely speechless.

Todd put his head in his hands. "Discussion, Chase. For fuck's sake, discussion first."

"I am discussing it. What the hell else am I doing? There are words and they are being directed at Haley. Discussion."

"More like word vomit pouring from your mouth, but it's done now. So," Todd gave me that intense look again. "Do you want to date us both, Haley?"

Haley

"So how about we take you out to dinner on Monday evening as a first date?" Chase asked.

"No can do. It's girls' night Mondays at Tiffs."

"Does Brandon join in with any nail painting?" he asked.

"No," I giggled. "Brandon is usually at the gym, or he goes for a beer. We used to have a girls' night every Monday when the girls both lived here. It was a tradition."

"Well, we could do something similar?"

I shrugged. "Thanks, but it wouldn't be the same.

It was chick flicks and moaning about men basically, oh and gossip from work. We will probably stop doing them soon because everyone's moving on with their lives."

"Why don't you still have them here on a Monday? We can make ourselves scarce. If we are going to be in a relationship, it would be healthy for you to have some time with your friends to be able to kick back and relax."

"Chase, we haven't even taken her on a date yet."

"Haley?" Chase came over to me and put his arm around me. "When we came for the interview, did you think to yourself, these guys will be great roommates, or these HOT guys can move in anytime because I can perve at them all day?"

"Kinda the second one to be honest."

"I have nothing further, your honor," Chase said to Todd.

"I would love to be able to move girls' night back here if that was okay with you two. Half the time Tiff's doesn't have any clean mugs or plates. I like to prepare snacks etc. It's fun."

"That it, it's settled then. From tomorrow evening, we shall leave you to your friends and then Tuesday night we are taking you on a date. Where would you like to go?"

I sucked on my lip while in thought. "Could we go back to the Italian restaurant I went to on my first disastrous date with Malcolm? It was really nice in there. I would like to wipe my memories of being there with him and replace them with some new ones."

"Done. Call and make reservations for eight-thirty." Chase commanded. He so made me laugh.

We spent the evening ordering yet more takeout and watching game shows. I felt so comfortable with these guys, like I had known them forever. The thought of getting to know them intimately made my stomach bubble with both excitement and anxiety. The risk was that we could ruin the happy roommate situation we had going on, but then, what the hell, there were other roommates, and to be honest if this didn't work I would probably go join a convent anyway.

"Look, Todd, she's smiling, and the contestant just said she recently lost her husband. I do believe our Haley is daydreaming about our huge cocks."

"Shut up," I yelled at Chase, and picking up a cushion I whacked him with it in the chest.

"If you want to knock the wind out of me, you need to whack me with that fat ass, not a tiny cushion." Chase grabbed me and pulled me across his lap.

"Stop it, Oh my god, Chase, what are you doing?"

"I am having a feel of this lovely ass." He gave it a slap.

"Ooh, it is so bouncy. Come and have a feel, Todd."

"Leave the poor woman alone." Todd stood up. "Come on, we are off to bed."

Chase stood me back on my feet. "Remember where we left off for Tuesday." Then he winked and they left me in the living room.

At Green's the next day I couldn't help but keep smiling to myself because I had two gorgeous men taking me out the next evening, and also, I might be having some dirty, hot sex. At last!

I noted that Malcolm kept watching me with a narrowing of his eyes. I ignored him and kept tapping into my computer, making notes for a presentation I had to make tomorrow afternoon.

A colleague called me to help with the photocopier and when I got back Malcolm was near my desk. Fortunately, I had all my documents password protected so the only thing he could have looked at was my cell laid on the top of my desk.

"Something you need, Malcolm?" I asked.

"No, not at all. I was just wondering how you were getting on with King Park. Only I have been speaking to a couple of the developers."

This didn't bother me. I knew Arthur Green, our owner, would not like Malcolm going directly to the developers. The developers went through Arthur. It was ultimately his say so. My meeting tomorrow was with Arthur and the main developer, but Malcolm didn't know that.

"Ah, that's fantastic. I also have a meeting about the development tomorrow."

"You do? Well, I'm very pleased for you. Let the best man or woman win, yes?"

"Indeed." I gave him a tight smile. "Will that be all then, Malcolm? I am very busy."

He backed away in his dark black suit looking like a retreating slug. I couldn't believe I had ever entertained the thought of dating him. I picked up my phone. I had a message from Chase.

I called Leonies. Table for three booked for 8:30pm. Todd and I look forward to enjoyable discussions about our deal!

. . .

The message box was marked as already open. I smirked to myself. If Malcolm was as pathetic as I thought he would be, my date tomorrow would be even more fun.

"Haley, baby. I missed you, bitch." Kayla bent down and ruffled the top of my head.

"It has only been a week. Get off me and get in the kitchen. You can get that wine you brought with you opened."

"Yes, Miss." She saluted me.

"How are things anyway?" I asked her. Kayla looked pretty as a picture. The sun had brought out her freckles and she had a healthy glow to her usually milk-white skin. She was wearing a floral tea dress and looked stunning and I told her so.

"Why, thank you." She did a twirl. "The dress is down to a lovely little vintage unit near the gallery and the healthy glow is due to nude sunbathing in the back yard and lots of sex."

"How is the gallery?" I asked, diverting her from the subject of sex until Tiff was here too.

"Amazing. Daniel has had interest in a picture

we all did together called Submit. I think his career could be about to explode."

"That is amazing for him."

"I know. The guy works so hard. His paintings are selling so quickly right now and people are on a wait list for his works. He has been offered ridiculous amounts of money for commissioned works but refuses now to paint portraits. He wants to paint what he wants and while people are waiting to buy whatever he produces, why not?"

"Why not indeed?"

"Hi, girls." Tiff walked through the door and planted herself straight onto the couch. "I am fucked and not from Brandon. I have been all over the place today. Sold a condo in Queens and a brownstone at Upper East Side."

"Just stay away from King Park."

"You so have that in the bag."

"Not according to Malcolm."

"God, I hate that man. He does nothing but stare at my tits."

"Tiff, we all stare at your tits, darling, they're huge," Kayla added.

"Not like him. He's a slimeball."

"He will get what is coming to him. I shall make sure of it. I am a firm believer in karma," I told them.

"Right, let's eat because we have tons to gossip about."

The poor chick flick never got played that evening because we didn't come up for air. Tiff told us that she and Brandon were going to try for a baby which brought tears of joy to us all. Kayla was so obviously happy with her home life and new career helping sell art. She said she didn't miss Green's at all, mainly because there the boss didn't call her up in the middle of the day for a massive sex marathon. Tiff and I thought of old Arthur Green with his bald pate and pot belly and made a mock heave. The guy was lovely, and around sixty-two years of age.

"Well, ladies. Tomorrow evening, I have a date," I announced, followed by my breaking out into a beaming smile.

Tiff and Kayla exchanged a look.

"What was that look all about? Aren't you pleased for me?" I asked. "I haven't even told you who it's with yet."

"Haley, babes. All your recent dates have gone to shit. We are worried rather than excited."

"Well, I have high hopes for this one because I know them already."

"Well, we know it's not Malcolm, so who is it with?" Kayla asked.

"Chase and Todd."

Tiff squealed while Kayla's forehead creased. "Chase and Todd."

"Yes, I am taking a leaf out of your books, and I am going out with two men at the same time."

"Fuck me," Kayla said. "That didn't take you long."

"I am so happy," Tiff said. "I kinda set the situation up. Henry knows them."

"Ahhh, so have they been part of the club scene?"

"I think so," Tiff said. "I guess you'd know more about that than me though, Hales."

"I'll ask them tomorrow on our date." I scrunched up my nose in excitement.

"So they're okay with sharing you?" Kayla asked. "Only it can become problematic. People get jealous. We had some issues at first. Parker can get very jealous at times."

"Well, that's something we'll have to work out, but they're together, Kayla. To-ge-ther. I'd be their female."

"An MMF? You're a fucking unicorn."

I scratched my cheek. "I'm a what?"

"A unicorn. Some people don't like it being called that so don't say it out loud anywhere like the club if you go, but it's a term for when bisexual men seek a female partner to have their babies, I think. Something like that anyway."

"And they said unicorns didn't exist and yet I may become one. Can I get rainbow colored hair?"

"That's My Little Pony, not a unicorn. Now, anyway, don't get carried away. See how the date goes. No harm done if you decide to change your mind," Tiff said.

"Fuck them first," Kayla said. "Then decide."

"You are so... oh my god, so... Kayla, sometimes," Tiffany groaned.

"Well, what happened to you Tiff. 'See how the date goes'. You turned up to the condo and fucked Henry's brains out without a second thought."

"Yes, but this is our little Hales."

"Stop being shortist," I giggled. "I'm only a month younger than you and two months younger than Kayla."

"Indeed, sweetheart, listen to the voice of experience." Kayla winked.

"So, what should I wear tomorrow?" I asked them. "They already know what I look like at my best and my worst. Do I still make an effort?"

"Absolutely," they both said in unison.

"It's a date. You dress up for the date just as you

would any date. Let them know you are willing to make an effort for them," Tiff said.

"Seriously fuckable underwear underneath the dress. Lace, as see-through as possible, but no peepholes or crotchless on a first date. Leave that for the second when they have already seen everything. Just a tease first time around."

I glanced over at Tiffany and took in her face as she looked at Kayla like she couldn't believe what she had just said. For a minute I imagined being in a room with Chase and Kayla together and I burst out laughing.

"What's so funny?"

"I just miss you ladies. I'm looking forward to a possible new future, but Monday nights have to stay forever you two. Promise me."

They both agreed to the promise and then something Kayla said earlier came to the front of my mind.

"Kayla. Earlier, you said something about a painting. That you all did it together. What do you mean? Have you become an artist too?"

"Christ, no." Kayla guffawed. "The three of us covered ourselves in paint and fucked on a canvas. Something I said gave Daniel the idea." She looked at our faces. "I know it sounds gross, but seriously, the picture is amazing. It's like our love displayed across the canvas. We did two and our other one is up on the living room wall."

"Well, look at that, Kayla might be maturing. Love displayed across the canvas," Tiff mimicked.

"Yeah, right, those are Daniel's words. I focused more on how well hung the men were than the canvas."

We rolled our eyes and laughed.

CHAPTER SIX

<u>Haley</u>

I'd felt strangely nervous all day. Although I'd kept telling myself I was just going out to eat with my roommates and to not think past that, I couldn't help it. I was wondering if I had made a huge mistake. Why hadn't I stuck to my original plan and gone to the club? Malcolm kept looking at me and smirking too which was pissing me off. I didn't have the energy to deal with his crap today. I was so nervous about the date tonight that my meeting with Arthur and the developer went like a dream. My presentation was immaculate.

I could tell Arthur was pleased. His face stayed relaxed throughout the meeting, and he didn't remove his jacket. If Arthur got tense, he got hot, and the jacket came off. The developer, Elias King, took me by surprise. I didn't know what I expected but it hadn't been a good-looking older man. He looked to be in his mid-forties with a sprinkling of black and gray stubble to his chin, and salt and pepper hair, spiked on the top. Most men his age wouldn't get away with that hairstyle, but he did. The pull of his shirt across his chest suggested he kept in shape. When we first met, his handshake had been firm and his hands soft, an indication that he may have started out in construction but now his business was conducted in boardrooms.

"I want someone I can work closely with on this development. Someone I can trust implicitly. I anticipate most of the properties will sell off to wealthy clients... clients who may not want others to be aware of their purchase. At this price range they could be, how can I put it, *choosy*, with their requirements."

"Haley handles many of our more exclusive residences. That's why I felt she would be a good fit for your development," Arthur commented.

I smiled. "I've dealt with many wealthy clients

and *choosy* requests. Obviously, I can't give you details as it's all entirely confidential, but I can assure you that your potential buyers will all be handled with the utmost discretion."

"Well, I'm very happy with what I've seen here today, Arthur, and I would like to accept Haley as my realtor for the development. Haley, my PA will be in touch to arrange for us to meet at the development, so I can show you around personally. I know you've visited before, but I'd like to ensure you know my vision for the place. King Park, is, in my mind, a unique development."

"Of course." I nodded. "I will wait to hear from your assistant. Thank you for allowing me to take on your development. You have my promise that your vision will be carried through. I'm looking forward to working for you."

"With me, not for me, Haley. No one I work with is my subordinate. I hate bosses who make their staff feel like they're somehow inferior."

Arthur clapped him on the back, taking me by surprise. "That's because your father brought you up right. I can't tell you how much I miss him. Haley is a superstar. You'll not have a finer realtor."

Arthur turned to me. "Thank you, Haley."

I got up to leave.

"Ah, just one more thing," Elias announced. "Can we not announce yet who is leading the development? I have another little deal happening where they might be put off if they know they haven't got this as part of the package."

"We'll leave it until you give us the go ahead," Arthur said.

"My lips are sealed," I told Elias. His mouth twitched as I said it. Surely, he wasn't flirting with me a little?

I had left the meeting and headed straight into the ladies bathroom. Checking no-one was around I'd squealed and done a little dance. I had got the development! *Fuck you, Malcolm*, I thought. I was going to have to try very hard not to do a little dance in front of his face with an accompanying smug grin.

Speaking of the devil; I hadn't even been back at my desk for ten minutes before he sidled over.

"You look nice today, Haley. Not that you usually don't, but you look extra nice today. Have you been, or are you going anywhere nice? I noticed you left your desk earlier."

"Not that it's any of your business, but Arthur wanted to check in with me about something."

His jaw tensed. "About King Park?"

"You're obsessed with that project. Not everything centers around it, you know? There are other properties to sell."

"Yes, but Elias King is a billionaire. To work for him could be to set yourself up for life. Word on the street is he's going to set up his own property management company, so he can keep it in-house."

"Well, I wouldn't know about that, and I am perfectly happy working here at Green's, so if that is all, I have work to do."

"Fine. Catch you later, Haley." He gave me that smirk again. I would have liked to slap it off his face.

I got home and went straight to my room to prepare for my date. I decided on a Nine West navy-blue, fit and flare dress that skimmed over my ass. It was sleeveless with a round neck and had a brown belt that cinched in my waist. I added some Michael Kor's 'Becky' dress sandals to my feet to give me some height, and grabbed my MK 'Mercer' clutch. My make-up was all smoky eyes and a red lip, and my dark hair was fixed up in a messy bun with a few stray tendrils around my face. I did the mirror shuffle where you tried to see yourself from all angles and I was pleased to see that I'd cleaned up quite well. I headed out to the living room to wait for my dates. Todd had agreed to drive us, saying that he was fine with not having a drink that evening.

"Cancel the restaurant, let's just take her to bed," Chase yelled out, jumping up and walking around me. "Fuck, Miss Martin, you look HOT."

"Chase. She is going to run back to her room in a minute," Todd scolded him.

"No, I'm not. I am totally used to him by now." I giggled. "You both look very nice yourselves. Anyone would think you were involved in property development," I winked.

"Do you really think sleaze ball will turn up tonight?" Chase asked.

"I would put money on it," I told him. "He has been smirking at me all day and he definitely read that text."

"Well, we have had an idea and we think you will love it." Todd gave me a wink back. It was nice to see Todd's more playful side. He was a lot more serious than Chase, but I just thought he took a bit longer to warm up to people. "Your carriage awaits, Mademoiselle," he added, and with that, we left the apartment and made our way to the restaurant.

Leonies was a mid-sized restaurant decorated in black and white with fifties movie posters on the walls and chandeliers hung from the ceilings. Black gloss tables had the obligatory candle on them, and the lighting was dimmed and had an orange glow to remove some of the starkness that the monotone color scheme would usually display. Todd pulled out my chair for me, a black leather cushioned back and seat alongside a silver-colored frame. Then he and Chase took their own seats opposite mine.

"Oh, it looks like we are interviewing her, I'll move," Chase said and he moved to sit to my left.

When the waiter came to take our order, I looked across at Todd. "Todd, if I ordered a half bottle of champagne would you be able to have one glass, only we are celebrating tonight."

"Yes, one would be okay." He looked at me, waiting for me to elaborate.

"Are we celebrating our threesome?" Chase asked. The waiter's eyes almost fell out of his head.

"Stop tormenting the wait staff," Todd chided. The waiter looked at us and laughed as if it was all a big joke.

I saw Chase's face tighten. I'd never seen him annoyed or angry before. The waiter took our drink order and then gave us some time to peruse the menu.

"I'm not ashamed of who we are, Todd," Chase spat out.

Todd sighed. "Neither am I, but we aren't in a threesome, Chase. We are here on a date with a beautiful lady who might be uneasy with how 'out there' you are. So just rein it in a little, okay?"

"Fine." Chase huffed. "You are a beautiful lady, Haley. What are we celebrating, darling?"

"It is totally hush-hush, but I got the King Park deal." I almost squealed the last three words, my excitement had yet to disperse.

"That is amazing," Chase said, hugging me, his previous annoyance gone in a flash.

"Congratulations, Haley. Much deserved and we look forward to that holiday," Todd added.

"Oh my goodness, yes. We can have a vacation after I've sold them all, to a place like paradise." My smile got wider than I thought was physically possible.

Our food orders were taken and we just continued with the same comfortable, cozy conversations like we had back at the apartment. The champagne made me more confident and I brought up the subject that had been on my mind and making me nervous for most of the day.

"Listen, guys, about our potential threesome situation. When we get home can we head to the bedroom? I would like to get that out of the way." I held up my hand. "I know that sounds completely unromantic but I'm nervous. You know my inexperience, and well, basically, if I can't be who you want me to be, then it's best we know straight off; you know, whether or not we are compatible."

"Ah, Hales," Chase said, adopting the nickname my friends gave me. "We will absolutely take you to bed when we get home, but do not have any worries, we are going to teach you how to do the sexy stuff until you are so good you could hire yourself out."

"Yes, Chase. Mr. Romantic there. Haley, it is not our intention to teach you how to be a prostitute. We will go back, head into the bedroom and see how it goes. Just know we are both nervous too. It is a huge step."

I breathed a sigh of relief. "Thanks, guys."

"Haley." The voice I expected came from behind me. "Imagine meeting you here."

"Malcolm. Wow, what a coincidence. What brings you here tonight?"

Malcolm's eyes flitted over the table. "I just popped in to make a reservation for a date. You know, I like this place. I was passing by, so I thought I'd book in person rather than calling." He looked at Todd and Chase. "Oh, sorry, I apologize. Am I interrupting something?"

Chase leaned over offering out his hand. "Chase Collins and this is Todd Ross."

Malcolm moved over to shake Todd's hand. "We've just invited Haley out for dinner. We're part of King enterprises. I don't know if you've heard of us? We are negotiating on behalf of Mr. King."

"Oh, absolutely." Malcolm was almost fawning. I was surprised he hadn't dropped to his knees. "Your development is one of the most exciting concepts I've seen in a long time. Haley and I have been working closely on forming the best plans in taking your development forward, haven't we, Haley?"

If this had been a real business meeting, I'm not sure what I would have done at his underhanded tactics. I was a quiet woman, and confrontation was not my thing. Malcolm had completely taken advantage of that fact.

"Really, well, would you like to join us? We have just eaten our main meal, but perhaps we could interest you in dessert and a glass of wine?" Todd asked.

Chase leaned over to me and mumbled under his breath, "He will be getting his just desserts."

Malcolm took a seat. "Oh, you have had some champagne. Were you celebrating something?"

"No," Todd lied. "I am just rather partial to the fine stuff. Shame you didn't arrive earlier, then you could have joined us in a glass."

"Not to worry, I will just stick to my usual beer," Malcolm said.

Over my dead body was he having any of my champagne anyhow.

Malcolm chatted on about his ideas for the development for a solid fifteen minutes before Todd stopped him.

"Sounds amazing, Malcolm. I'm sure we can come to some arrangement. Now can I talk candidly with you about the building? This is highly confidential and other than Haley you must not speak of it. We have taken her into our small circle and not even Arthur Green knows this."

Malcolm's eager eyes opened wide, and he shuffled closer to Todd. "Anything we talk about is strictly confidential. You have my word."

"So, part of the funding behind King enterprises comes from the adult entertainment industry."

Malcolm's jaw dropped for a split second before he quickly recovered himself.

"We are hoping that some of our wealthier investors will choose one of the King homes, and we're also going to keep one for filming high class movies. We've been speaking to Haley this evening and think it would be beneficial for you to come to our current movie set, see what we do, how we do it and then use that vision on the home Mr. King intends to keep for that purpose. You may or may not see some of the investors on that day too. I must point out that if any of this becomes public knowledge, Mr. King has advised me to do whatever is necessary to shut down the leak."

You couldn't miss the tenseness in Malcolm's shoulders at those words and when he spoke a slight tremble underlaid his voice.

"I won't say a word."

Well, who'd have thought it? Todd seemed to be rather enjoying pretending to be some kind of mob member.

"So, we will be in touch with Haley about you coming to see us. Would you be okay with attending on a Saturday, probably outside of usual office hours so that your employer isn't suspicious?"

"Of course, we will do everything necessary to assist you in this deal. Won't we, Haley?"

"Of course," I stated, and I raised my glass which was still partly full of champagne. "Here's a toast to a successful conclusion to our arrangement."

Everyone clicked glasses, with only Malcolm not privy to the double meaning of my statement.

We stayed silent on the subject until safely back in Todd's car.

"The fucking mouth on that man, Haley. I don't know why you didn't just let me and Todd beat him up at the back of the restaurant."

"Because he's not worth it," I stated. "I knew he'd show up tonight. I told you he would. He's a back-stabbing bastard. Thank you for winding him up tonight. I'll tell him it was a sham after I'm allowed to say I won the development."

"Don't say anything just yet, Haley," Todd said, winking at me through the rear-view mirror. "I'm not done with him. He's coming to the studio. I have plans to get him out of your life for good."

"You've gone all Godfather. Are you going to put a horse's head in his bed?" I laughed.

"No, but I do have plans for his head," Todd's dark eyes glistened with mischief.

"I'm seeing a totally other side to you tonight, Mr. Ross," I told him.

"You're going to see all our sides when we get home, darlin'," Chase added, and my stomach fizzled with excitement.

"Oh, she just trembled. Don't be a nervous girl, we'll be gentle," Chase said.

"I'm not nervous," I told them. "I actually can't wait."

CHAPTER SEVEN

Haley

I unlocked the door to our apartment and Chase and Todd followed me inside. As I naturally would, I headed into the living area. Todd walked over to the kitchen and took a bottle of red from the cupboard.

"Whose room would you like to go to?" he asked me.

"Let's go to mine. Mine is the largest," I replied.

"Chase, come grab some glasses," Todd commanded. It would appear Todd was totally in control of the situation, and I was happy to let him take charge.

We walked back down the hall and I opened the door to my room. I didn't know if either of the guys had had a secret peek in my room when I hadn't been around. Looking at their faces, I saw Todd taking in all the décor: my cream walls, gold satin curtains and matching bedding, along with my ornate framed mirror and ivory colored vintage style furniture. "It's like a Princess lives in here." He smiled. "Princess Haley of Dyker Heights."

"At your command," I bowed. His eyes flashed with desire. The first time I had seen a hint that he liked me in that way.

His complete opposite, Chase had flopped back on the bed like it was his own room, so there were no prizes for guessing that he'd seen my room before. "Move over," I told him. "There's more than you needs to get on the bed."

My curtains were drawn from when I had got changed earlier. I switched on my nightstand lamp and Todd switched off the main light. He sat at the other side of the bed and poured the wine into three glasses, handing one to each of us.

"Let's get more comfortable."

Todd stood and removed his jacket, hanging it over the back of my chair. Then he unbuttoned his shirt and repeated his actions. His torso was lean but muscled, with a slight smattering of dark chest hair that ran in a narrow trail down his stomach and into the waistband of his boxer briefs. He had narrow hips and a defined V and I was desperate to know what was beneath the boxers. His cock bulged underneath. He sat back on the bed and rested his head against my headboard.

"I'm too lazy to strip, Hales, you're going to have to help me," Chase said with a fake whine.

I smiled as he sat up. As usual, he'd discarded his jacket to the floor in the living area, so I helped him unbutton his shirt revealing light golden skin and a six-pack to die for. As his hair was fair it wasn't as noticeable where it ran down under the waistband of his trousers, but his abs and stomach were ripped and moved like beautiful waves on water. I had an overwhelming urge to trail my tongue all over him.

When we'd removed his shirt, he threw it down at the side of my bed. I began to unfasten the button on the waistband of his pants and then pulled down the zipper, although it was a struggle given the package underneath. Chase raised his hips up off the bed so that I could tug down his pants over his legs and off. Joining in his messy ways, I also threw his clothing on the floor. I reached over and took a sip of my wine as my mouth had gone dry.

"Now my boxers," Chase said. "I find myself incapable of doing a thing. You're going to have to do everything for me, Haley."

There was no doubt in my mind as to what he was insinuating. After my eyes saw his cock it was time to introduce my mouth. I swallowed; this was where it could all go wrong.

"Don't be nervous," Todd said gently. "We're here for you. We're not going to embarrass you or criticize you. We're all here to have a good time."

I smiled at him and then brought my focus back to Chase.

I hooked my fingers in the waistband of his boxer shorts and tugged them down, freeing his cock.

"Now take your time, Haley. We've got all night," Todd directed. "Hold it in your hand, look at it."

The cock in front of me was huge. It looked quite wide and was certainly bigger than any I'd seen before. After discarding his underwear, I held him in my hand. He was warm, and his dick hardened while in my grasp. I pulled the head back in my hand, looking at Chase for direction, and revealed a pink tip.

"Run your fingers over me, Hales." I saw a spot of pre-cum bead from the slit in the top of his head and I rubbed my finger into it and slid it around his glans.

"Just a moment. Let me grab something that will help," Todd said, and he left the room.

"See, we're not going to bite you," Chase said. He placed his hand over mine and rubbed it up and down his shaft. I found his rhythm and then he let go, letting me continue. He leaned back watching me. "Don't be afraid to go harder," he said.

Todd returned to the room clutching a tube of lube. "Strawberry flavor," he informed me. "But at first it will help your hand slide nicely down Chase's cock."

He poured a small amount into his hand and then came closer on the bed. I let go of Chase's dick and watched as Todd placed his hand around it, massaging in the lube. "Show her how hard she can go," Chase requested.

Todd gripped Chase's dick firmly in his grasp and pumped up and down with vigor.

"Wow," I said. "I would never have tried to go that hard. I'd be afraid of hurting you."

"You've done hand jobs before, right? With your old boyfriend?"

"Yes, as a prelude to the main event, but I just got him hard. I wasn't fierce like you are."

"Here, take over." Todd took his hand away and placed my fingers around Chase's cock.

Feeling more confident, I pumped my hand firmly up and down his shaft, eliciting a groan from Chase that made me stop.

"Why are you stopping?"

"I'm shocked. I never got that reaction before."

"Keep going, babe. I'm getting into it."

Chase leaned back against the pillows once again and closed his eyes, while I pumped my hand up and down his girth until my arm ached. I swear my arms burned so bad I could have cried. Todd saw my struggle.

"It is hard work, and that is why we move on to using a different body part. Now you are going to take him in your mouth, okay?"

I nodded.

"So, teeth covered, just slide him right in. You do not have to do what you have just done with your hand. Think gentle this time. The heat of the inside of your mouth is going to stimulate him, the lube will help you to slide him in and out. Feel free to wet your mouth with some wine too if you think it will help."

"I'm okay. My mouth isn't dry."

"Okay, so hold him at the base with your hand.

Now slide him into your mouth and back out, gently. That is all you are going to do at first. Get used to his size."

I did as instructed. Chase's dick filled my mouth. The taste of strawberry lube made the experience more pleasant and he did actually slide into me. I remembered Todd's words. Slide him in and slide him out. Each time I did it, I tried to take more of him in.

"Now, don't attempt to deep throat him, you will just gag. A little tip is to let the head of his cock gently hit the roof of your mouth. It feels very similar to being deep throated."

I tried to communicate with my eyes that I understood and this time when I took him into my mouth, I let the tip gently bump the roof of it. I looked over at Chase and saw his mouth was open and his breathing had hardened. My God, I must have been doing something right!

I let him slip out of me a moment. "I'll just take a drink."

"You are doing great, Haley." I found Chase staring at me. "It's hot thinking of your relatively virgin mouth around my beast."

Todd chuckled. "Are you still all right carrying on, because I can take over at any time?"

"No, I'm okay." I took a gulp of my wine. "I want to keep going. Tell me what else to do."

"Exactly what you are doing, but now suck me more. Do what they say and pretend I'm a popsicle," Chase said.

"That didn't work out so well for me with a real popsicle," I stated.

"Why was that?" Todd asked.

"I ice-burned the inside of my mouth."

Chase chuckled. "I assure you mine isn't frozen, so you'll be burn free unless I get you on your knees on that carpet."

I grasped the base of his cock once more and leaning forward I slid him into my mouth, sucking. I moved my head up and down, letting his cock bob in and out of my mouth. Then, feeling emboldened, I did what Tiff had advised me, and I took him out of my mouth and rolled my tongue gently across and around the top of his glans.

"Now, just increase the pressure of your sucking and the speed but keep to a steady rhythm. Be guided by Chase and how he thrusts inside you, okay?"

I nodded and then it was all systems go. I imagined myself to be a sophisticated seductress who had done this many times before. I placed my grasp firmly around his base and as I took him further into my mouth, I also slid my hand up and down his shaft. I sucked harder and then I increased my pace. Chase began to fuck my mouth gently and guided by him I increased my speed and pressure.

"That's it," Todd encouraged. "When Chase gets ready to come he'll tell you and you can choose to swallow or let him come out of your mouth and I'll take over at the end."

I held him out of my mouth one last time. "I want to do the whole thing."

"Okay," Todd said, and he moved to rest back against the headboard himself. He picked up his wine and settled in to watch the show.

I pumped Chase's cock and sucked. Feeling more confident with a real cock in my hand and mouth and no pressure to perform, I tried different things: swirling my tongue, sucking, cupping his balls. I figured if he didn't like any of what I was doing he would tell me. Soon Chase's rhythm appeared more focused. His breathing intensified, and his hand came toward the back of my head, guiding me to take him a little further into my mouth. The speed picked up and soon I was bobbing my head up and down for all I was worth while I sucked. My cheeks started to hurt, but I didn't care, I was seeing this through to the end.

"Oh, fuck, oh, Haley, fuck, I am gonna come."

I felt his cock tighten and his balls pull back and then with a groan he emptied his cum into me, filling my mouth. I swallowed every last drop of the salty milk and then carefully, using my hand at his base, I placed his cock against his stomach. Then I reached over and took a drink of my wine. I hoped it wasn't bad etiquette after swallowing his cum, but the taste was unusual, and my throat still felt dry.

"Bravo, Miss Martin." Chase sat back, a satisfied smirk on his face. "You did a perfect blow job. Nothing whatsoever to be ashamed of. Nothing to correct you over. You made me come and I am one highly satisfied customer."

"Chase, you're making her sound like a call girl again."

"Oh, yeah. Sorry, Hales. Tell you what, I won't pay you." He winked.

"I can't believe it. I did it. Thank you for being so patient with me." A beam set across my face and the relief that I'd performed well was as good as having had a solo orgasm.

"Can I do you too?" I asked Todd.

"I would love a blow job, Haley, but first you

need to rest your mouth, so I think it's time we took care of you."

I bit my lip, not knowing what to expect. I was still fully dressed at that point. Chase got me to stand up and he lowered the zipper at the back of my dress and pulled it up over my head, before handing it to Todd to put on the back of the chair. So he could be tidy sometimes! I stood in front of Chase facing Todd in my underwear. I'd purchased a new matching set in a silver lace with tiny crystals and sequins embroidered into the fabric, so they sparkled when they caught the light. My bra was a push-up style which held my small bust up and made it appear a little fuller than it actually was, whereas the thong let my ass cheeks out in all their glory. And that's what Chase was looking at right at this moment. His hand brushed down my right ass cheek before giving it a squeeze. "Hell, woman, your ass is delectable."

Todd leaned over toward me and offered his hands. I took them in my own and he drew me back to the bed where he laid me down facing upwards, my head resting on the pillows. I noticed his boxers bulged with his erect cock straining at the material. Todd dropped one of my bra straps off my shoulder and then the other. I lifted myself up slightly so he could unhook me. My breasts freed and my bra joining my dress, Todd looked over at Chase who came over to join us and one man sucked on one of my nipples, while the other feasted on the other. I thought I'd died and gone to heaven. I'd become so horny while I'd been sucking Chase's cock, but it was nothing on how I was now as I felt my juices soak through my panties, while I watched a blond-haired man and a brown-haired man feasting on my tits. Their hands were everywhere except *there*, trailing down my body, my thighs, up the side of my waist. Lips left my breast and kissed and sucked at my neck. Then Chase moved back and watched as Todd leaned down to my panties and pulled them down and off my legs. He eyed me greedily as he pushed my thighs apart.

"Pussy. You see as much as Chase and I love each other, we also love pussy."

He nestled between my thighs and I felt the warmth of his breath near my core. Then he took a leisurely lick up my slit which nearly had me come up off the bed.

"Oh my fucking god."

My experience of having oral sex was almost virginal. As I'd said before, Liam despised it, and to be honest he'd made me feel like it was dirty and shameful. Todd's tongue wrote an entirely different story directly on my cunt as he trailed it up my crease, teasing my clit and then went back to my crease where he stuck his tongue directly into my entrance.

I felt barely conscious, overtaken by sensations I had never experienced before. My hips rose to meet his tongue fucks until I felt a concentration of tiny, almost electric shocks, alongside a wave of complete elation. My orgasm exploded. I'd never come like that before in my life and I shook with the intensity as my juices squirted over Todd's face. He licked his lips until he'd taken in every part of my cream.

I sat up against the headboard panting. "Oh my god, I never... I never experienced anything like that before."

"He's so good with his mouth and tongue," Chase agreed. "Girl, you just had your world rocked."

"I really did." My face broke out in yet another megawatt smile. "I never knew it could feel like that."

"Well, hopefully, that's the first of many," Todd replied, moving to lie back against the headboard.

Without being prompted, I grabbed the waistband of his boxer shorts and yanked them down, displaying his cock in all its glory. It was hard as a rock, veins standing out and the head of his cock was a deeper color than Chase's, more purple than pink. His cock in itself was darker in skin tone. I marveled at the difference between their dicks. Todd's dick was also huge. I would actually say it was bigger than Chase's, but not as wide. Without hesitation, I took him in my mouth. I repeated all the things I'd done with Chase's cock, but this time I was more confident. I leaned over him, my ass high in the air while I brought him closer to climax. Chase stood at the side of the bed near the headboard, watching while he fisted his own cock a little and then he moved onto the bed where Todd took Chase's cock in his mouth. The room filled with the sounds of ecstasy. Groans, moans, sucking, licking. Todd was the first to come, erupting into my mouth. He tasted saltier than Chase, but I guessed that could have been due to the fact that we'd not used the lube. I sat back and watched as Todd's mouth bobbed up and down on Chase's cock with practiced precision. I stared, taking mental notes on how he moved his mouth around Chase's shaft. When he was about to come, he withdrew and sprayed his spunk over Todd's face. Todd licked it off his lips as it dripped down. Watching two guys really was hot.

Chase turned to me. "Well, Haley. I think that's

enough for our first evening together. We didn't want to rush you into anything too quickly, so we'd talked in advance and decided that we'd stick to oral sex tonight. Now I don't know about anyone else, but I'm satisfied, relaxed, and beat. I need my bed."

Todd stretched, leaning to grab his shirt and wiping his face. I might have been tired, but I watched those muscles as they rippled. Then he swung his legs off the bed. "I'd better go because otherwise I'm going to fall asleep right here, and as Chase says, it's too early for some things yet. Sleep well, lovely Haley. He leaned over and kissed the left side of my cheek. Chase followed suit, leaning over and kissing the right side.

They left and I didn't know whether they went to their own rooms or shared. I wasn't sure what they would do now that everything was out in the open and we were looking toward a ménage. The word made my lips curl into a smile. Two men at once. Two men all for me, well, apart from each other. Tonight I had performed two successful blow jobs! I couldn't wait to tell the girls. I quickly removed my makeup and took a shower, then I dressed in my pajamas and crawled into bed. I was exhausted and up again early in the morning. It wasn't until I was almost asleep that I realized I hadn't been kissed. My pussy lips had met Todd's mouth but I'd yet to crush lips against either Todd or Chase. I guessed that happened when intimacy deepened. I was pleased everything was going to be given time to develop, but at the same time, I couldn't wait for more.

CHAPTER EIGHT

Haley

I was pleased to discover that Malcolm was out showing properties all day and that I could go about my own day without seeing his ego-bloated face.

I was about to go show a property myself and had just grabbed my purse when the phone on my desk rang.

"Good morning, Green's Realtors, Haley Martin speaking."

"Good morning, Miss Martin, it's Alexandra Cross from King's. Mr. King has asked that I get in touch with you to arrange for him to meet you at the King Park development."

"Oh yes, of course, let me just bring up my electronic diary. I sat back at my desk and tapped on my keyboard until the main diary displayed. It was easier than trying to stare at the app on my phone, which made everything hard work.

"Okay, I'm in. When would Mr. King like to see me?"

There was a pause. "He wondered if you could meet him this afternoon at 2pm."

Of course, he did. He was a billionaire. They didn't wait for meetings. If they wanted to see you, you jumped. I looked at my itinerary for the day and hoped Tiff wasn't too busy and could fit my client in. "That would be fine. I will meet him there at 2pm." I knew I would be there by 1:45pm at the latest. Never would I leave a man of his importance waiting.

"You'll be met at the gates to the development and be given a visitor's badge and anything else you need. He looks forward to seeing you then."

"Thank you, Alexandra, please pass on my regards and tell him I look forward to meeting him too."

I put the phone down and called Tiff, passing on

my client's details for that afternoon and then I drove home as quickly as I could because although I looked smart, I didn't feel I was dressed well enough for meeting a billionaire.

At 1:39pm I arrived at the gated development where I was given a security badge and directed to a car park. From there a man in a suit introduced himself, and handing me a hardhat took me into the main entrance of the development. The vast mansion had been separated into four, five-bedroomed residences, each with their own entrances. The only thing connecting them all was one vast marble-floored hallway. There were two apartments upstairs and two downstairs, each with their own long hallway that led down to their grand entrances. It was homes within a home.

"If you'd like to wait here, Mr. King will be with you shortly."

I thanked him and while I waited, I strolled around the vicinity. The building work appeared to be largely completed. The façade of the building was limestone clad and each apartment had its own balcony or private patio. The lawns outside were almost the size of a small park and meant that residents would maintain a degree of privacy, maybe not always from the three other owners, but at least from the general public.

"Miss Martin. Thank you for joining me at such short notice."

I startled. I was so lost in the architecture of the building, I hadn't realized the man himself had arrived.

"My apologies." He placed a hand gently on my shoulder. "I didn't mean to startle you."

My skin shivered under his touch, and I moved further away from his body, wrapping my arms around my shoulders. "It's fine. I was just admiring the beauty of this building."

"Yes, I made sure my architect knew that the outside of the building was to be maintained. It's the inside that has been modernized. Come and I'll take you into the one apartment that has been completed."

I'd only seen the completed apartment in photographs. The last time I'd visited, the front of the building had been wrapped in protective materials, there had been scaffolding everywhere and the apartments were finished in terms of the main construction but had yet to be decorated.

"If you'd like to follow me, Miss Martin."

"Please call me Haley. Miss Martin makes me sound like an old maid." Elias laughed.

"You're hardly that. How old are you if it's not too personal a question? You look around the same age as my daughter. She's twenty-one. By the way, call me Eli, that's what my friends call me and I'm sure we're bound to become them with you handling this development."

"I'm twenty-four, Eli. You have a daughter? Is she interested in joining the family business?"

He laughed again; it made his face light up. He really was an attractive man, although far too old for me. "No. No. Unfortunately, she takes after her mercenary mother, doesn't believe she needs to work for a living and likes spending my money. Are you married, Haley?"

I blushed a little. "No, I'm not."

"Don't worry, I'm not propositioning you. I just wanted to offer some advice. If you become wealthy, ensure you have a pre-nup because there are people out there who think they deserve a large part of your wealth when they didn't do a thing to contribute toward it."

"Your marriage was a success then I take it?" I quipped.

"Well, let's put it this way. I never made the same

mistake again and don't intend to. Marriage is not for me. I prefer the single life, and golf."

He opened the door to one of the downstairs apartments. It was bright and airy and had all the amenities one would expect from a luxury residence. It was beautiful.

"I can't wait to begin selling these residences. They won't be available for long, Eli."

"Well, that pleases me. If we work well together, Haley, I'd very much like Green's and yourself, in particular, to represent King's on the property front."

"Oh." My forehead creased. "A colleague of mine felt you were going to expand into the business yourself, cut out the middleman, so to speak."

"I considered it at one point, but I don't have the time. Why mess around when Arthur Green has been in the business as long as he has and knows how to sell. Would you consider being the first point of contact for my businesses? It would take you away from a large portion of the day-to-day real estate selling of Green's."

"It sounds fantastic, and I have a friend and colleague, Tiffany, who would also be a good back up for myself."

"As long as it's not that wretched man. What was his name again? Oh, Malcolm. If that man leaves a message for me one more time to speak with him directly, I'll have to speak to Arthur about him."

I smirked. "Oh, don't worry about Malcolm. I'm taking care of it."

A mischievous glint appeared in Eli's gaze.

"Really? Please do tell. I may be too old for you, but I'm not too old for a little mischief."

It would appear that Eli and I were going to get along just fine.

CHAPTER NINE

<u>Chase</u>

"I think last night went really well, don't you?" I asked Todd for about the thirtieth time. We'd called for lunch at a small café in Brooklyn before we headed back to the studio.

"I've already told you my answer." Todd exhaled. "It was a great night but it's extremely early."

"I already love Haley," I said. "Instalove. The minute I met her, I knew, just like I did with you."

"We dated other women for three months before we got together." Todd rolled his eyes.

"Only because I was too scared to approach the dark, brooding male, who I presumed was straight as a ruler. Had I known you were interested I'd have had your cock in my mouth within a minute of meeting you."

He'd heard this all before, but I was telling the truth. Haley was special. I felt it. We'd known her for a few months now as a friend and she was becoming more than that.

"I really hope it works out because I'm over trawling Club S for pussy," I told Todd. "I'm almost thirty. I'm getting too old."

"So, the fact I'm thirty-one means I should have stopped by now then. Put myself into sex club retirement?" Todd raised an eyebrow.

"Oh, you know what I mean. You have the stamina for things, the determination. I'm bored and over it all. We meet someone, half the time they lie about their true identity. We very rarely see them again. Sometimes one of us likes them and the other doesn't. In the meantime, people are watching and getting their rocks off while we try to enjoy ourselves. I used to find it hot, but now I'm jaded. I'm a jaded bisexual man, Todd. I want to come home at night to my man, and our woman. Maybe travel, have a family.

He clasped my hand. "It's what we both want. It will come with time. I was over Club S a long time ago. I just don't want you to scare Haley off. You know how full on you get."

"But that's who I am. There's no point me pretending to be someone else. The relationship needs honesty from the start. Well, apart from the bit where we show Malcolm around the studio." I sniggered.

"That sniveling suck-up bastard is going to get everything he deserves." Todd's voice dripped with venom, but it told me all I needed to know about Haley. He deeply cared for her too.

Saturday morning was the day we'd arranged for Malcolm to visit the studio. There was no way we were allowing him to come to our real place of business, so instead, we gave him the address of the brownstone we'd rented for the week to film a new set of movies. We liked to think ours were more sophisticated pornos with a storyline, though I imagined even though we spent hours making sure we had the best movie possible, most viewers probably skimmed past the whole introductory phase and went straight to the pussy shots. Our small team was already there with everything set up. The bedroom was filled with camera equipment, and the bed made. Our actors for the day Guy, Angie, and Rod (not his real name, but named for a reason) were in the kitchen, along with half the crew, enjoying a bit of breakfast before filming started. I'd had a word with Rod, told him what I had planned for Malcolm, and with the promise of a bonus he shrugged his shoulders, totally on board with the plan. I guess it was just another cock to him.

Haley had arranged to meet Malcolm for the 'studio tour', and just after eleven, I heard a cab pull up outside the house. A few minutes later the doorbell rang, and I went to answer it. The show was on the road.

"Welcome to the shoot." I shook both their hands. "Please come in. Everyone is grabbing some breakfast. I'll quickly show you around, tell you what to expect and then feel free to get a coffee and watch the action."

Haley gave me a secret wink, whereas Malcolm's eyes were wide as he took in the townhouse.

"Not what you were expecting?" I narrowed an eye at Malcolm while trying my best to keep a friendly tone.

"I honestly didn't expect movies to be filmed

somewhere so, well, nice. I kinda thought it would be in some seedy basement apartment somewhere."

"All our shoots take place in the most sumptuous surroundings and our crew and actors enjoy fantastic working conditions. We run a company with a fabulous reputation."

"Oh, yes, I wasn't insinuating—"

I cut him off. "Let me show you around as we really need to get on with the shoot. Time is money."

I walked them around the townhouse. On the parlor level, there was an enormous living room with a stained quarter sawn white oak floor throughout. Underfloor heating in every room meant our actors' feet wouldn't get cold during all the standing around. High ceilings and tall windows, along with the cream painted walls meant the house was bright, airy and perfect for filming. The bedroom we were in today was gorgeous. A large room with the bed situated at the top, with ample floor space around for all the cameras.

After Haley and Malcolm had grabbed a coffee, we went through to the bedroom to make a start. An hour later our actors were still acting out the beginning scenes of a housewife being caught in the bedroom looking out at the hunky gardener and were still fully dressed, something we expected having made so many movies, but our two guests were shuffling around on their feet appearing quite bored.

"Were you expecting things to happen a little faster?" I asked them both.

"Yes," Haley replied. "I don't know how you don't fall asleep, it's so boring."

"Haley," Malcolm scolded. "You can't say that to these businesspeople." He coughed and turned to me. "It does take longer than I anticipated, however." He adjusted his tie and preened like a peacock. "The email I received yesterday from Mr. King stated he hoped I enjoyed the experience and made the most of it."

I nodded, knowing full well that Elias King also wanted Malcolm to get what was coming to him for being such a dick. When Haley had told us he was happy to go along with our charade and would even send the email to back us up, I'd been amazed.

After a couple more hours, the actors' clothes were off and we were into the scene.

"We need the cat light. Cat light please," the director yelled.

A runner went off to the back of the room and wheeled over the massive light which was so bright you felt it could melt your eyeballs. It was set up to shine right into Angie's pussy, hence the director shouting cat light. We actually called it the pussy light but reverted to cat if we had visitors.

I watched Haley as she watched the scene acted out in front of her. It was a ménage but an MFM one. I wondered if she was getting turned on. Malcolm was, he'd moved his laptop case in front of his pants. When the scene was finished, Todd approached. "Okay, Malcolm if you stay with Chase, he'd like to talk business. Haley, are you okay to come with me and grab some lunch?"

Haley nodded and neither Todd nor I missed the look of smug satisfaction that crossed Malcolm's face and how he gave Haley a look of sheer triumph.

"So, if you'd like to follow me?"

I walked into another smaller bedroom with a double bed and a desk and a couple of chairs. I indicated for Malcolm to take a seat.

"I'm going to come right out and say it, Malcolm. You're a natural. We want to offer you a job with us."

"A job? An actual job? Not the development contract?"

"No. A full paid job. However, as I'm sure you can understand, we have a lot of enemies, and for collateral we therefore have to obtain guarantees that none of our staff give away our secrets."

"I fully understand. I'll sign any confidentiality agreements."

"It's not that simple, Malcolm. You're a man, like myself. We can make a lot of money, and when people make money it can go two ways. They can get enemies out to crush them, or they can enjoy themselves so much they can become complacent. Either way, we do something here, a little off the norm that means we, to date, have never had a problem."

"Anything. You name it."

"We need to film you sucking a man's cock."

Malcolm almost choked. "What? Are you kidding me? I can't do that. Jeez, man."

"Well, Haley is currently being offered the same deal by Todd, so I guess we'll see who wants the job more." I got up to leave.

"I'll do it," he blurted. Shaking his head as if he couldn't believe his own words. "How long do I have to do it for? Does he have to, you know, in my mouth?"

"God, no. Literally like suck on it for a minute. Just enough that we have it on film. Then it gets locked away in a security deposit box and will never be seen again."

"Okay, can I get it done with quickly? Oh my god, fuck, oh erm, sorry about that. I can't believe I'm going to do this."

"I know." I put a hand on his shoulder. "When I had to do it, I found it hard." I turned away then because I wanted to laugh at my own joke. I wished Todd and Haley had been here to hear it.

"I'm filming it on a handheld. There'll just be me, you, and Rod. So no massive audience. Now, don't worry. Rod is used to having all different people on his cock. It's not going to turn him on, you're not gay from doing it. It's just a business transaction, okay?"

Rod entered the room completely stark naked, his massive twelve-inch cock in his hand. He stroked it, keeping it hard.

"Okay, Malcolm. On your knees, please. Time is passing quickly and we have more filming to do."

Malcolm swallowed and dropped to his knees. Then he closed his eyes and opened his mouth. Rod pushed his dick in between his lips. Neither of us said a word. We just watched as Malcolm sucked Rod's cock in and out of his mouth for about a minute.

"All done. Thanks, Rod," I shouted. Rod nodded, winked at me and left the room, taking the handheld with him. He had instructions to take it straight to Todd.

"The bathroom's down the hall if you want to freshen up," I informed a green looking Malcolm. "Then come join us for some lunch."

Malcolm nodded and then ran down the hallway looking like he was going to vomit.

I went and found Todd. "Everything good?" I asked him. "Perfect and backed up," he said. "All ready for us to wrap up this little situation for good."

Malcolm came downstairs and walked into the kitchen. He refused all offers of food, but he walked over to Haley and whispered something in her ear that made her eyes flash with fury.

"So, while it's just the four of us here. I'd like to announce that earlier I offered Malcolm a job," I announced.

Malcolm preened again.

"And if you would still like the position of the part of the wimpy computer nerd in our next production, we would be very happy to have you."

"What?" Malcolm choked. "There must be some mistake. You offered me a job at King's."

"No, I didn't," I corrected him. "I said you were a natural and we wanted to offer you a job with us, as in, the studio."

Malcolm's face drained of all color. "I sucked a man's cock."

Haley burst out laughing. "And we have it on tape, you fucking asshole."

He turned to her, looking in horror.

"That's what you get for trying to home in on my account, Malcolm, and for being one of the most unlikeable people I have ever had the misfortune to meet. You're despicable. Did you not think I'd notice that you read my private text message? Unfortunately for you, you made an incorrect assumption. I wasn't meeting business partners. I was meeting my live-in partners. Meet my lovers Todd and Chase."

Malcolm's jaw dropped. "Both of them?"

"Yes," Todd answered. "Both of us and we can assure you that she is fucking top of the class at blow jobs and sex. Your dick didn't inflate because it lives mainly on your head."

"So, this was all a fucking joke?"

"Oh no. We run a very, well-respected adult entertainment business, and if you don't want your video leaking on one of our associates' amateur channels, you'll put that cock firmly between your legs, get on with your own work at Green's and leave Haley and anyone else you annoy at Green's the fuck alone. Now get out," Todd shouted.

Malcolm didn't need to be told twice. He ran out of the brownstone. We all high-fived each other.

"Party at ours tonight," I declared. "Lots of alcohol and sexy shenanigans. We have lots to celebrate!"

CHAPTER TEN

Todd

Malcolm had gotten on my last nerve and I was pleased he ran off because I was so tempted to hold him by his lapels and beat the shit out of him. My temper rarely flared but when it did, it took a lot to get the heat to dissipate from my body.

After the shoot, we went out to eat, and with the knowledge of catching a cab home, I'd had wine with my dinner. I was satisfyingly full of food, but the burn was still there and I knew one way I could channel it that would be of benefit.

As soon as we got through the door, I pushed

Haley against the wall, parting her thighs with my knee. My mouth crushed on hers, my tongue seeking entrance into her own warm mouth. Her lips parted with a sigh and her tongue met my own.

"Come on, Chase. Go get the lube and join us." I lifted Haley up and kicked open her bedroom door. I stripped her of her clothes, Chase by now assisting, and then we stripped off our own quickly until we were all bare and ready for action. Chase leaned over Haley, placing his hand under her head and lifted it letting his mouth meet her own. I watched as they kissed.

"I can't wait tonight, Haley. Are you ready for me?" I asked her.

Chase let her mouth go and she gasped, "Yes."

I held my rigid cock in my hand and lined it up at her entrance. She was soaking wet, her juices were spilling out onto the bed. Without hestitation, I pushed inside her. Fuck, I needed that. To feel encased by the warm walls of her pussy.

She moaned.

I pulled out of her to the tip and then pushed in again. Her legs came up to wrap around me, to take me deeper. Her head was flung back.

"More. I want more," she whispered.

I gave her more. Plunging in and out of her wet

heat, the tension and rage I'd been carrying around all day went into every thrust. Chase went back to kissing her. Haley couldn't get enough. She arched to meet my thrusts and she mewled through Chase's kisses. Her hand came up to grasp his cock and I watched as she milked him. It wasn't rhythmic. Trying to co-ordinate kissing, hand-jobs and fucking wasn't some kind of orchestrated performance. It was raw. Chase broke the kiss to concentrate on the hand on his cock and her hand stopped as I rammed into her so hard she must have seen stars.

"Todd, I'm gonna—"

I flicked her clit with my fingertip as I continued to fuck her until her pussy contracted and she came all over my cock and fingers. Her pussy continued to throb against me for several seconds. I hadn't come myself yet. I wanted to wait.

"Wait for a minute," I told her, and I took Chase's hard cock into my mouth. With years of practice behind me, I placed my tongue up over the back of my throat, taking Chase into my mouth, making him feel like he was fucking the back of my throat. He grabbed my head as he guided me in a rhythm he would get off on. As I felt the giveaway signs that his come was approaching, I backed off, looking up at him and shaking my head.

"No. We fuck. Haley, move further left and turn on your side facing left."

When she'd done it, I directed Chase. "Move behind her."

I moved behind Chase. Chase brought his hand around the front of Haley and began to finger her clit, alternating with plunging digits into her pussy. "So wet, Haley, I hope you're ready for me."

She wriggled her ass at him indicating that she definitely was. "Oh that ass," Chase groaned. "Wiggle it again, baby."

He lined up his cock with her pussy and entered her slowly. This time we would take our time. I moved in behind Chase and lubing up my dick and his puckered hole, I slowly edged into him pushing through his outer ring. He moved back against me until I met the known resistance of his inner ring, waiting until it relaxed and let me push my cock in further. Chase gasped as I pushed all the way into him, my balls slapping against his ass cheeks. I held his hips as I followed his lead with my movements, mirroring my fucks to his fucking of Haley. Now we were all in perfect orchestrated motion. A trio of lovers searching for their crescendos. Leisurely strokes turned into animalistic movements and grunts as the pressure built and then Haley climaxed which set off a chain reaction. Chase spilled his load into her tight pussy and I jerked violently as my cum spurted inside Chase's ass.

We laid back against the bed spent. But this time we didn't leave. We took turns to visit Haley's bathroom, then got back in the same positions, curled up and went to sleep. My anger was no more. Malcolm was insignificant. Haley was with us and we would protect her for as long as she allowed.

CHAPTER ELEVEN

Haley

I almost asked if we could have girls' night on Sunday. I was absolutely bursting to tell the girls what had happened over the past week. So much had changed. After our date and my lesson in oral, they'd left me alone until the Saturday night. I'd been surprised. I'd kind of expected a non-stop fuck-fest. I wasn't sure whether I admired the fact they were respecting me and taking their time or whether to just go to them and demand they fucked me. I was becoming sex-crazed. Me! Little Haley Martin. The quiet girl who didn't do sex, who wasn't very good at sex, now had had two amazing experiences. I knew now that it wasn't only down to me. The lovers I'd had were useless in bed and along with my lack of confidence it had meant that I'd struggled to develop any kind of sexual skill. I also knew now that it was all about to change. Bring it on, I thought. I couldn't wait for more. Saturday had rolled around to Monday and although there'd been a lot of making out, we'd not had sex again. Instead, Todd and Chase had insisted on taking me to the movies and bowling on Sunday. They were determined to date me. They were off to the gym tonight and then had got Brandon to agree to them hanging around at his apartment, while I borrowed his wife for the evening. By the time Kayla and Tiff arrived, I was a bundle of nervous energy, had drunk half a bottle of red wine already and was feeling rather dizzy, but manic.

"Come in, come in," I'd shouted at both of them, and they'd taken a seat at the dining table while I served some spaghetti and poured the last of the red wine into their glasses.

"What the fuck is going on with you, Haley? You're like a bloody jack in a box," Kayla said.

I squeezed my ass through the gap between the table and my chair and sat down, twirling spaghetti around my fork. "I did it! I did two blow jobs and I've had sex with both Todd and Chase!" Then I squealed because I was just so damn happy and excited about the whole thing.

Tiffany high-fived me and then Kayla took her lead and did the same. Tiffany beamed at me. "I'm so happy for you. Spill it. What was it like? What did you do? Did you see them fuck again? Are two men really hot together?"

"Jesus, Tiffany. One question at a time and give the girl time to eat her spaghetti or she's going to choke on it," Kayla chided. Then she turned to me. "Haley, eat the damn spaghetti so we know what happened."

"Okay, so the first time I just did blow jobs, but they were so kind and patient. It wasn't like they took pity on me or anything, it was still super sexy, but they gave me words of encouragement and advice, and it worked. I used some of the hints and tips you two had given me too, but it was so much better to not suck and lick a piece of hard plastic or a mushed-up banana." I made a gagging face. "Then after we set up Malcolm—I'll tell you about that in a moment — we came back here, and Todd was all masterful and pinned me to the wall. I felt like I was in a movie."

"Yeah, rewind this movie a minute. What did you do to Malcolm? I thought he'd been quiet this week," Tiff said.

"We tricked him into giving a male porn actor a blow job on camera and then told him where to go."

Kayla spat out her wine. "Holy shit! How did you pull that off?"

I filled them in on all the details of the porn shoot and how Eli King had also been part of proceedings.

"Wow, that guy really does know how to piss people off," Tiff said.

"And now he knows how to suck a dick." Kayla laughed. "That's hilarious. Are you sure you don't have a copy on hand that we can watch?"

"No, Todd actually wiped it, so it couldn't accidentally get out anywhere, but Malcolm doesn't need to know that, does he?" I giggled.

"Haley, you are becoming quite the minx. Tiffany, where's our innocent little Hales gone?"

"I think she's gone forever judging by the wide smile that's almost permanently etched onto her face. Now you know why we got so hooked on ménage. It's so decadent having two guys at once."

"Yes, but Hales has even more holy hotness because then her guys bang each other. Mine won't cross swords, I've asked them. Parker said I could go back to sleep because I was fucking dreaming."

That made me laugh because Kayla was a force of nature, and Daniel, her older partner was a quiet man. With Parker, she'd met her match and had someone to make sure she didn't get too carried away; though I'm not sure what she could do worse than some of her past antics like being discovered having a threesome in the kitchen by her own mother and having sex on canvas. She was loud and brash and I loved her like a sister.

"Do you miss it?" I asked Tiffany.

"No. Honestly I don't. It's in here." She tapped her temple. "But I love Brandon. I cared for Henry. I thought at one time I might have loved him, but I didn't. I barely knew him, whereas as time passed Brandon and I just become closer than ever. I'm ready to start trying for a family now and Brandon himself exhausts me. That gym training gives him Olympic-level stamina. I swear sometimes I have to pretend to be asleep when he comes to me for round four in a day.

"Well, I've only seen Todd and Chase that time when I spied through their door; and then when we got together Friday night, we were in like a spoon situation, so I couldn't see them then. I'm really looking forward to actually watching them fuck each other in front of me, up close. I swear I had no idea two guys together would turn me on like it does.

"I'm so happy for you, babe. I hope it works out." Tiff leaned over and gave me a squeeze.

"Well, thank you, Tiff. Because if you hadn't spoken to Henry and engineered these two hot men into my apartment it wouldn't have happened, and I'd still be a sexual nervous wreck trying not to gag on fruit and vegetables. I had to move onto carrots. I never want to see a banana up close again as long as I live."

"To cocks in place of bananas," Kayla lifted her wine and toasted.

"To cocks in place of bananas," Tiff and I sang back.

"So, in other news. I totally won the King development. I met the big man himself over there and I'm waiting for it to be announced to the team."

"Babe, that's amazing," Tiff said. "I knew you could do it. You deserved it with all the effort you put into the plans. Well done."

"When I met Eli, he spoke about putting more

business Green's way and having me as a contact person. I also told him about you as my back-up."

"Wow, this is so exciting."

"Sometimes I miss working for Green's," Kayla admitted. "Not the work. I actually prefer the art world, but I miss seeing you girls every day and talking about the latest gossip."

"That's why we must never let our Monday's stop. Not even when we have children. That's what fathers are for, and in mine and Kayla's case there'd be two fathers so no excuses for a lack of childcare."

"My god, are you seriously thinking of starting a family with Todd and Chase?" Tiff said.

I shook my head. "It's far too early to decide anything like that, but I want to keep a positive outlook. If things carry on as they are—and we've all lived together for several months now—then why the hell not?"

"Let's have a final toast. To friends and ménages." Tiff said. "Seeing as both things have made us all very happy."

We raised our glasses and clinked them together.

When they left, Tiff sent the men back home.

"Did you have a good time? Is your tongue worn out from all the gossip?" Chase asked.

I stuck it out at him.

"Hmmm, seems okay to me. We'll test it later though to make sure."

He sat down on the couch. "First though tell me everything. They did nothing but talk about baseball over there. Please tell me all the girly gossip. Was there sex talk? Did you tell them I had a huge cock?"

Todd came in as Chase delivered his last sentence.

"Dear God," he said, shook his head and went to grab a beer.

CHAPTER TWELVE

<u>Haley</u>

A week later and Eli had given the go ahead to announce the deal. Arthur and Eli came into the office having called a staff meeting. Arthur had a large bouquet of flowers in his hand and Eli a bottle of a very fine brand of champagne.

"Everyone, Mr. King has an announcement to make which is of great benefit to Green's. Please, can we have your attention for a few minutes?"

People stopped what they were doing and looked over at the impressive and commanding man standing before them.

"Thank you, Arthur. As you may or may not know, King's has expanded into the property market during the last year with a vision to develop a brand of elite housing. I am pleased to announce today that not only have we chosen a person from the team to represent the King Park development, we have also, as King's Enterprises, signed on the dotted line for another three developments which will all be coming Green's way in terms of sale and management. So, today, I'd like to formally announce that Haley Martin will be our key link person between Green's and King's."

"Congratulations, Haley," Arthur added. "And if you'd like to come forward, we would like to present you with these flowers and a bottle of champagne as a token of our appreciation."

Everyone cheered and clapped. Well, everyone except for Malcolm, who left the room. You see Green's was mainly a family-style business and although we may get a little jealous of each other's good fortune and landing of big commission deals—after all we were only human—in the main we cheered each other on as every success meant Green's went from strength to strength and guaranteed us future employment.

I took the offered gifts and shook both Arthur and Eli's hands and then I went and sat back down.

Eli spoke again. "While we congratulate Haley today on her new role, it goes without saying that it's the team who attracted me to Green's. You are led by a fine gentleman—"

He was interrupted in his speech as everyone cheered Arthur. After the whooping and cheering calmed down, Eli carried on. "The business I intend to bring to Green's will make an impact on everyone's workload, so as a thank you for you all being so accepting and encouraging of our new business arrangements, I'm hosting a free bar tonight at my bar in Manhattan. We have the private room held for us at eight and there will be food also for you. Please come along to PlayKing's tonight and let's let loose and welcome the weekend in style."

Everyone whooped and hollered again.

"Thank you, Eli, for this opportunity. I promise I won't let you down."

Eli smiled. "Haley, I'm feeling like a new man lately. Obviously, I needed the new direction with the business. I was becoming jaded and then your youth and vitality must have rubbed off. I'm feeling invigorated. What happened with Malcolm?"

"He's left me alone ever since. I guess I can't ask for more than that."

"Actually, you can," Arthur interrupted, holding a piece of paper in his hand. "Malcolm just quit. He'll be gone immediately. Thank God. He was the one bad apple at Green's, a poisonous red one." He chuckled. "Now, I usually don't condone drinking at work, but I have another bottle of champagne in my office and I think we should drink to throwing out the old and bringing in the new."

And we did.

I returned home elated about the new direction of my career and the disappearance of Malcolm from my life. Eli had told me to bring the guys along to PlayKing's that evening. I walked into the living room to find Chase almost bouncing off the walls.

"Haley, we have news."

"I have news too." This was probably obvious owing to the fact I had flowers and champagne in my hand, but hey, I wanted to join in with the announcements.

Todd interjected. "Haley, you go first."

"What?" Chase looked like he'd been told there was no Santa.

"Haley?" Todd prompted.

"The deal was announced today. Eli has invited us out to PlayKing's tonight for an open bar, and Malcolm quit. It's been a fucking fabulous day."

"Oh, honey, it's about to get better. We sold the business," Chase almost screamed.

"What?"

"The movie business. We were made an offer we couldn't refuse by someone who wants to take what we do and expand it. We got our retirement pot and I'm not even thirty. You know what that means, babe? The vacation is on us. Forget your bonuses, we want to take you, our treat. You pay for massages and stuff if you want to contribute."

Todd shook his head and walked over to kiss my cheek, then took the flowers and champagne from my hands and put them on the countertop. "Huge congratulations, Haley, and Malcolm is gone, really? That's the best news I heard all day." He looked over at Chase, "even better than our deal."

"You are so full of shit sometimes, Todd." Chase pouted. "Anyway, no time to waste. Let's get ourselves ready for the free bar. It's time to paarrttyyy."

. . .

And party we did. We let loose, we got a little wasted, and we danced the night away even though there was no dance floor in the bar. Eli came over briefly, although most of the time he was still conducting business. I met his personal assistant, Alexandra, who followed him around all night like his shadow. Eli was blissfully unaware of the look of pure longing and hero-worshiping that was on her face. I had hesitated to point it out to him in case it complicated their business relationship, but the alcohol got the better of me.

"Eli, I think your PA wants more than a business relationship with you."

Eli's eyes widened, and he gave a half-laugh. "You're mistaken. Alexandra is twenty-six, just five years older than my daughter."

"I know want when I see it and she wants you."

"Well, I'm too old for her."

"What did you say to me? I'd brought some youth and vitality to your life. She could bring some more." I winked.

"I'm going to forget we had this conversation," he said, winking back at me and he walked away.

It wasn't lost on me that as he did, he looked

directly at Alexandra, who came running over to see if he needed anything. He did, and I hoped he realized that sooner, rather than later.

I turned around to see my men—yes, I realized I saw them as that now, my men—-wrapped around each other dancing.

I walked over and tapped them on the shoulders. "Is there room for one more?"

"Always," they said and let me in their circle.

A month later, Chase and Todd had handed over the business to the new guy, Aiden Hall. They came home one evening with Chase holding a new movie in his hands.

"Are we watching your last porno tonight?" I asked him.

"Oh, we are," Chase grinned. "I think you're going to like it."

We curled up on the sofa, me in the middle of the guys, and Todd pressed the remote bringing the movie to life on screen. The story unfolded—-my story-—beginning with a woman being told she was no use in bed and leading on to her love affair with two men. I broke down in tears.

"Haley, did we make a mistake? We didn't want

to hurt you. We wanted to show you how we felt you'd changed. How beautiful you are," Chase said, looking at me in alarm.

"That's why I'm crying," I replied. "I feel like I'm in a fairytale sometimes; like it's not real. You took me and made me be this confident woman I am now. You really did change a caterpillar to a butterfly."

"Except we got you to spread your legs not your wings," Chase quipped. It broke through my tears and I started to laugh.

"That you did," I said. "And I'll be forever grateful."

"Ooh, how grateful?" Chase said with a wink.

I dropped to my knees. "Let me show you."

CHAPTER THIRTEEN

Haley

Six months later

Todd and Chase had stayed on as paid consultants for a while at their newly sold business until Aiden Hall had someone trained to take over. I had sold all of King Park within the first week of the apartments being available and was working closely with Eli on a number of new developments.

But this week, we were on vacation at our dream

destination. We'd arrived in St Lucia, staying in a hotel with views of the Petit and Gros Piton mountains. Our suite was modern and well furnished with a beachfront location and 24-hour butler service. That night we had a table set out on the beach in front of our suite. It was set up underneath a wooden cabana: just a roof and four pillars, with curtains that floated in the breeze but gave us a feeling of privacy. Lanterns gave us light and kept it all very romantic.

"So, here's to our first night in St Lucia." Todd raised his glass of red wine.

"Yes, let's toast with strawberry cordial," Chase said with a wink in my direction.

"Shut up." I gave him side-eye, but then the edge of my lips curled in a tell-tale smirk. It was impossible to be mad with Chase for longer than thirty seconds.

"So, what's everyone thinking we should do tomorrow?" Todd asked.

I looked over at the other cabana directly to the right of our suite. "I'm going to have a massage."

"Oh, I'm definitely joining you on that one. What do you think, Todd?"

"I think I'm going to have a game of golf. I haven't played in a while. I'll leave you two to gossip while you're being kneaded."

We relaxed in the warm breeze. It was decadent and romantic, being spoiled as someone else cooked and brought the most delicious food to our table. The staff let us know they'd turned down the bed. There was one bedroom and a sofa bed, but we'd explained we only needed the bed. If our butler had any thoughts about our arrangement, he kept them to himself.

Thoroughly relaxed, we headed back into our suite for our first night in 'paradise', and we went through to the suite.

"That dress is beautiful," Todd said, indicating toward the maroon sundress I'd been wearing that evening. Then he walked over and flicked the thin strap off my shoulder. "But I prefer it off." He flicked off the other strap and Chase stood behind me and unzipped it, so the dress pooled at my feet. Todd pushed me back onto the couch, moved my panties to one side and slowly licked up my slit. His mouth fastened over my clit and he sucked gently, making my juices flow. His tongue continued to make leisurely trails up and down my slit, occasionally darting inside my pussy, making me moan.

Chase came up behind Todd, "My turn."

Todd left my pussy and turned on his knees to face Chase, who unbuttoned his pants and pulled down his boxers to reveal his erect cock. Pre-cum glistened on the end of his mushroom head. I watched as Todd took him in his mouth. Chase indicated for me to kneel up on the couch and I leaned over Todd, while Chase held the back of my head and kissed me, his tongue darting between my teeth. His other hand cupped my breast then caressed my nipple, while he moved in a steady rhythm inside Todd's eager mouth.

Chase withdrew his cock from Todd and told me to get on the floor on all fours.

"Todd, fuck Haley."

Todd moved behind me and positioned his cock at my entrance. Chase stood just astride my body facing Todd and again put his cock in the other man's mouth. Todd thrust inside my wet opening. I turned my head and could just make out where the men were. I wished we had mirrors in the room so I could watch our play, but instead turned back to the front, closed my eyes and lost myself to the sensations of Todd's huge cock pushing into me over and over again. Chase moved to one side of me when Todd's motions became more frenzied. I got onto my knees and Todd clutched my breast while he fucked my body hard until he came with a loud grunt, which took me over the edge. My cunt quivered as my orgasm rang out.

I turned back and rested against the sofa. "I want to watch you both," I told them.

We moved into the bedroom. Todd was soon hard again and he and Chase positioned themselves in a sixty-nine and took each other's cocks in their mouths. I found it so erotic, watching these two men, both their eyes closed as they pleasured each other, and I placed my own hand between my legs. As their fists held the other's cock at the base, I watched tongues swirl and mouths suck and listened to the slurping sounds, pops, and groans coming from the men I loved. Fuck, I realized. I did. I loved them.

My middle finger brushed against my nub gently, causing my core to drip out even more of my cream. I swept some up on my fingertip and rubbed it into my clit. It was almost like electricity was pumping through my body. Both of their dicks were otherwise engaged and I looked around quickly. I needed that feeling of fullness while I played. I wanted a cock, but there wasn't one free. I took note of the unlit candle at my bedside and reached for it. It was brand new. They changed the candles daily and it was tapered with a thicker base. I positioned it at my entrance and slowly pushed it in while I moaned, feeling it slide in comfortably thanks to my juices until it was almost the whole way in, with just enough at the base for me to grasp. I watched as I withdrew the candle from my pussy and then I pushed it back in. It was so dirty but oh so hot. Turning my gaze to the men, I watched their heads bob, their mouths working each other's cocks while I fucked the candle. I pinched my nipples with my other hand, stroking my own breasts and feeling my core quicken and pulse as if my mouth down there was frantic to reach its fruition. Chase came in Todd's mouth and without delay, Chase withdrew and concentrated on bringing his lover to his own climax, but while he did, he opened his eyes and he saw what I was doing with the candle. He didn't move his gaze. Instead, he worked Todd's dick while he watched me push the candle in and out of myself until I was fucking it hard and raising my hips off the bed. My other hand was pinching my clit. Todd opened his own eyes at this point and Chase moved him onto his side slightly so they could both have a view.

Chase's mouth frenziedly sucked on Todd's dick while they both watched as I fucked that candle like it was one of their dicks until I exploded all over it, sitting up and shaking, my breathing ragged, the candle still inside me. Todd spilled his seed into Chase's mouth, Chase swallowing it all down.

"I can think of another use for that candle," he said. "But first how about we share some more wine and catch our breath?"

Recovered, we returned to the bedroom and Chase got Todd to kneel up so that his torso rested against the wall at the top of the bed. Then he lubed himself up and pushed himself into Todd's asshole. "Now, let me enjoy the candle," he said.

I'd never been involved in any kind of anal play before, but I'd watched Chase and Todd together, so I rubbed plenty of lube onto it and then used my finger to smear some in and around Chase's anus. I let my finger push in and twist a little inside him. Chase wiggled back onto me, so I tried again with two fingers. It was a strange sensation. At first, there was a resistance but then his ass relaxed and my fingers went inside feeling the spongy insides of his inner walls. I could imagine a dick going in there and I decided that at some point in the not-too-distant future I'd like to try that too. I figured I'd let them christen my ass with their fingers first and work up to their dicks, seeing as they were so huge. If I hadn't seen them fuck each other I would never have believed such huge cocks could fit in asses. I removed my fingers and slowly pushed the candle in until it got past the tight band and slipped inside and then I slowly pumped it in and out. I matched my rhythm exactly to that of Chase's fucking of Todd and I noticed that Todd had his dick in his hand and was sliding his hand up and down his own cock to match the rhythm too. We were in perfect synchronization and as Chase sped up, so did we. I listened as his dick pumped and Todd groaned on every thrust. Todd's hand went up and down his cock so fast it almost made me dizzy and it made that slapping kinda sound as he did so. I wasn't sure how much Chase was enjoying the candle seeing as it was nowhere near the size of Todd's cock until I accidentally stopped using it for a moment, engrossed in Todd and Chase's fucking and hand jobs, and felt Chase push back against me with a definite hint to start again. Todd was the first to blow, shooting his load into his hand, his head falling forward, forehead resting against the wall. Then Chase went next, withdrawing his cock at the last minute so his cum sprayed in a jet all over Todd's rear. I removed the candle and threw it to the floor, then climbed up the bed and opening Todd's hand I licked it free of cum.

"Anyone feeling sleepy yet?" Chase asked. "Or shall we head for a skinny dip?" We all ran down to the water, cavorting and splashing each other. There was no one else in sight and it wasn't long before I felt Chase behind me, his hard dick bobbing in the water, hitting me between my legs.

"Don't tell me you're ready to go again?" I exclaimed.

"I'm always hard around you and Todd. I just can't stop. I need an anti-viagra before I have a heart attack," he said. Then he scooped me up and ran with me all the way back to our suite before unceremoniously dumping me on the bed.

"That's no way to treat our Princess," Todd declared as he walked back in, shaking the wetness from his head.

"So how should we treat her?" Chase asked.

Todd asked me to stand up and then told Chase to lie on the bed. His cock stuck straight up like a hoopla game.

"Now sit on his cock with your face facing the end of the bed, toward me," Todd directed.

"I feel like I'm being directed in one of your movies." I laughed.

"Haley, this is hotter than any movie we've made. That's fiction, this is real life."

I took hold of Chase's hard as a rock dick and raised myself above him before slowly lowering myself onto his rod. "God, that feels so good," I said. Then Todd got on the bed and began to tongue and finger my clit. "Holy fuck," I exclaimed.

The sensations from both of them were too hot for me to handle. I sank and rose on that huge cock with abandon while I clutched my tits in my hands, pinching my nipples. I could feel my ass bobbing up and down while I fucked him.

"Yes, yes, Haley, like that. Don't stop, please don't stop," Chase commanded.

I now had a hand in my own hair, holding it off my face while I rode Chase like I was at the rodeo. I almost yelled yee-haw I was enjoying myself so much.

Meanwhile, Todd's tongue and fingers continued their assault on my clitoris and labia.

"Oh, please, yes, right there, yes right there. I'm coming, oh god, I'm coming, oh, oh, oooooohh."

My juices squirted into Todd's mouth and dripped down Chase's dick. While my pussy contracted, I moved up and down on his rod as fast as I could until I sent myself dizzy through lack of oxygen. Then I felt his balls tighten and he emptied his load straight up into my pussy.

Todd knelt over me and jerked off furiously until he too let his cum flow until it mingled with ours.

After a few moments, I withdrew and collapsed back against the bed. "I can't do anymore. I'm exhausted."

"Me too," Todd said, lying at the side of me.

"Wimps," Chase quipped.

While we sat and gathered our breath, Chase went over to the freestanding large bath positioned in the center of the suite and ran the faucet until it was full of water to which he'd added a generous amount of bath soak. "Come and join me," he yelled to us both. "No sexy stuff. I can see I've worn you both out. Let me help get you clean so we can all enjoy a good sleep afterward smelling of the scent of vanilla with undertones of caramel," he read off the label. "Oh, that makes me want to eat ice cream."

"Come on, Haley, let's get in the bath. The faster we get in, the faster Chase will be quiet and we can get back to bed and sleep."

The bath was exquisite, the warmth of the water relaxing my newly aching joints and we took it in turns to rub each other's shoulders and wash each other's hair. We soaped up each other's bodies. There was nothing sexual about it, it was sensual. As we sat, limbs entangled, leaning back against the edges of the tub, I decided to make my declaration.

"Chase and Todd, I have something I want to say." I held up my finger in front of Chase's open mouth before he could make a sound. Now was not the time.

"I want to thank you for inviting me into your relationship. I realized tonight, that well, I love you. I love you both," I told them.

"I've loved you since the minute I met you. Didn't I say that, Todd?"

"Yes, yes you did." Todd agreed, smiling.

"Haley, I love you too. We love you."

It was the perfect end to a perfect day and we dried off our bodies and lay together in the most comfortable bed I'd ever been in. We definitely needed to ask the hotel where they sourced their materials, so we could have this heaven all year round.

It had taken me a while to find out where I belonged both sexually and romantically but there was no doubt in my mind that now I had found my two true loves and I couldn't wait to see what our future held.

THE END

You can read H, Aiden, and Eli's stories in The
Billionaire Series, starting with The Billionaire and
the Virgin (H's story)
Read on for a sneak peek...

THE BILLIONAIRE AND THE VIRGIN

Chapter One.

H

June 2004

"Henry, when can I take this blindfold off? I swear I'll trip over in a minute and squash the baby."

"A few more steps, honey, and there's no way I'm going to let you do anything that will harm a hair on either yours or our son's head."

I guided her further from the car down to the driveway until Veronica faced the door.

"Ready?" I asked. "I'm going to remove the blindfold, so it might take a moment to adjust to the light."

"Hurry, Henry. I'm so goddamn excited."

I removed the blindfold and my wife gasped. In front of her was the front door of a nine-bed house in East Hampton. She took a few steps back and swung around, taking in the enormous yard, then back to the front of the house. She was yet to notice the separate three-bed annex and when we eventually walked through the house, she'd see there was a pool house to the rear.

"Henry, what is this?" she asked. My wife was always cautious. She never assumed anything. Never took anything for granted.

"This, honey," I replied, taking her in my arms and stroking her honey-blonde hair. "Is our new family home. That's if it meets your approval once we've been inside."

"But it's so huge. There's only the two of us..." She placed her hands across her stomach. "For another five months, anyhow."

I kissed the top of her forehead. "Our son is just the start. Let's see how many of the rest of the seven guest bedrooms we'll be able to fill."

She laughed at that. Her green eyes glistened with unshed tears. The baby hormones had been making her very emotional of late. "You'd better take me inside to look at it then." She moved out of my arms and grabbed my hand instead.

I took her through every room one by one. Through the living room with its vast windows that flooded the room with light, with sea-blue couches reminding us that the beach was only a few minutes away. An archway led through to a dining room, with a mirror-topped table that seated ten, and then through again to a magnificent white kitchen. But of course, what I was now desperate to show her was our master suite—a large room painted white, with floor-to-ceiling windows adjacent to patio doors that led out onto our own private balcony with a stunning view of the ocean.

"Henry, this is too much."

"Vee, we came from nothing. Built ourselves up from rock bottom, worked our asses off, and now we get to enjoy the benefits of our investments paying off."

"I guess so." She looked out at the view. "And it sure is pretty. We get WiFi here okay though, don't we?"

"Yes, my workaholic wife. You'll be able to run your property empire from whichever room in the house you decide to turn into your office."

"I like to keep busy," she said and then she

clutched her head. "Ooooh." She gripped my arm. "Wow, that hurt."

"You okay?" I led her to the edge of the bed. Vee had always suffered with tension headaches—an unfortunate side effect of the stresses of running a billion-dollar business—but the last couple of days she'd been complaining more.

"I'm going to ring Dr. Anderson later," I told her. "It could be due to your blood pressure."

"You fuss too much," she said. "I'm just going to freshen up in the bathroom. I'll be right back."

"You sure you're fine?" I asked again and was given a narrow-eyed glare. I raised my hands in surrender. "Backing off."

"Good." She smiled. "I love you, Henry Carter, but I'm an independent woman and I can splash water on my face all by myself."

"I can't wait for you to see the bathroom," I said. It was enormous, with a free-standing bath and separate steam room amongst other luxuries.

Vee had been in the bathroom for a few minutes when I called out to check she was okay. Yes, I fussed; yes, she could just get used to it. When there was no response, I hurried over to the room, fully expecting her to chastise me once again for fussing.

But she didn't.

My beautiful wife was slumped on the floor.

I'd not heard her fall because the house was so damn large.

They told me afterward that even if I had heard her, I'd have been too late. An undiagnosed brain tumor had taken my beautiful wife. Our baby boy died too inside his mother's womb at eighteen weeks old.

I lost my wife.

I lost my son.

I lost my ability to love.

My world was gone and with it went my hopes and dreams.

Instead of celebrating life, we mourned the death of a woman taken too soon, and that of my son, taken before he even had the chance to take an independent breath.

I stood at the graveside with Vee's mother, father, stepfather, and her young stepsister. Amelia was just nine years old and spent the entire funeral inconsolable, wrapped in the arms of her parents. I stood beside Vee's father, who'd never remarried after separating from her mother.

"I'll never love anyone else," I told him.

"We'll understand if you do," he said, then he looked at his ex-wife. "But I never did."

I put the house straight back on the market and sold it to the first people who offered on it. I didn't give a damn what I got for it, I just needed it gone.

I kept the business going. I owed it to my beautiful wife to work my ass off to keep our property empire growing.

Years passed.

I had needs.

I visited a sex club, and I had my needs met, with no strings.

Never again would I marry or try for a family.

I bought the club and named it Club S.

Everyone thought Club S stood for Club Sex.

It didn't.

It stood for Club Stop. It was where I called time on my life.

ROMANCE IN NYC: Forbidden Bosses

Abandon

Exception

Confession

ABOUT ANGEL

Angel Devlin writes stories about bad boys and
billionaires. The hotter, the better.
She lives in Sheffield with her partner, son, and a
gorgeous whippet called Bella.

When not working, she can be found either in the
garden, drinking coffee, watching too much TikTok,
or daydreaming about her ideal country cottage.

She's a firm believer in living in, and enjoying every
moment and hopes her words bring you that
enjoyment. Let her know by leaving a review, joining
her newsletter, or dropping her a line via Facebook
or email.

Facebook page: https://www.
facebook.com/angeldevlinbooks

E-mail: contact@angeldevlinwriter.com